THE GIFTS OF CHRISTMAS

ANNA CAMPBELL

Serenade Publishing

ISBN: 978-1-925980-91-2

Cover design: By Hang Le

Print editions published by Serenade Publishing
www.serenadepublishing.com

THE CHRISTMAS STRANGER

At Christmastime, a stranger crossing the threshold means good fortune...

When Josiah Hale, society's favorite aristocratic architect, stumbles upon an isolated manor house in the middle of a snowstorm, he feels like he's entered a fairytale world. And Sleeping Beauty in this secret corner of Yorkshire is lovely, vulnerable Maggie Carr, surely a princess disguised as a humble housekeeper. Is Josiah her prince – or the man who will break her heart and leave her life in ruins?

But is the stranger's arrival lucky for the girl Christmas forgot?

Maggie Carr has worked as a housekeeper at isolated Thorncroft Hall since her beloved mother died five years ago. No matter how often she tells herself she's accustomed to being poor and alone, Christmas always stirs poignant memories of a time when she had a place in the world and a family to love. But this Christmas, a handsome stranger bursts into her solitary world and makes her feel like a desirable woman. Maggie has already lost so much to cruel fate. Now as the season advances and she finds herself in thrall to the man who challenges her loneliness and turns winter nights to sultry summer, what price will this irresistible passion demand of her?

Will the Yuletide enchantment vanish with the season's decorations? Or have Maggie and her Christmas stranger discovered a magic to sustain them through a lifetime of happiness?

THE WINTER WIFE

Will a chance meeting on Christmas Eve...

Alicia Sinclair, Countess of Kinvarra, cannot believe that fate has been so cruel as to strand her on the snowy Yorkshire moors with her estranged husband as her only hope of rescue. During their rare encounters, the arrogant earl and his countess act like hostile strangers. Now that Alicia has fallen into Kinvarra's power, will he seek revenge for her desertion? Or does the dark, passionate man she once adored have entirely different plans for his headstrong wife?

...deliver a second chance at love?

Sebastian Sinclair, Earl of Kinvarra, has spent ten wretched years regretting the mistakes he made with his young bride, but after long separation, the barriers between them are insurmountable. Until an unexpected encounter one stormy night makes him wonder if the barriers of mistrust and thwarted desire are so insurmountable after all. When winter weather traps Sebastian and his proud, lovely wife in an isolated inn, could the earl and his headstrong countess have a Christmas miracle in store?

PRAISE FOR ANNA CAMPBELL

"*The Seduction of Lord Stone* is romantic, emotional, sexy and funny. In fact, everything I have come to expect from Anna Campbell. I'm looking forward to reading the other Dashing Widows' stories." —*RakesandRascals.com*

"With her marvelous combination of humor and poignancy Anna Campbell writes in such a way that every story of hers has a special meaning and remains like a sentimental keepsake with those fortunate enough to read her work!" —*JeneratedReviews.com*

"*Lord Garson's Bride* is a well written and passionate story that touched my heart and sent my emotions on a rollercoaster ride. I particularly recommend this book for fans of convenient marriages, and those who enjoy seeing a deserving character find out that love is lovelier the second time around." —*Roses Are Blue Reviews*

"Campbell immediately hooks readers, then deftly reels them in with a spellbinding love story fueled by an addictive mixture of sharp wit, lush sensuality, and a wealth of well-delineated characters."—*Booklist, starred review, on A Scoundrel by Moonlight*

"With its superbly nuanced characters, impeccably crafted historical setting, and graceful writing shot through with scintillating wit, Campbell's latest lusciously sensual, flawlessly written historical Regency ... will have romance readers sighing happily with satisfaction."—*Booklist, Starred Review, on What a Duke Dares*

"Campbell makes the Regency period pop in the appealing third Sons of Sin novel. Romantic fireworks, the constraints of custom, and witty banter are combined in this sweet and successful story."—*Publishers Weekly on What a Duke Dares*

"Campbell is exceptionally talented, especially with plots that challenge the reader, and emotions and characters that are complex and memorable."—*Sarah Wendell, Smart Bitches Trashy Books, on A Rake's Midnight Kiss*

"A lovely, lovely book that will touch your heart and remind you why you read romance."—*Liz Carlyle, New York Times bestselling author on What a Duke Dares*

"Campbell holds readers captive with her highly intense, emotional, sizzling and dark romances. She instinctually knows how to play on her readers' fantasies to create a romantic, deep-sigh tale."—*RT Book Reviews, Top Pick, on Captive of Sin*

"Don't miss this novel - it speaks to the wild drama of the heart, creating a love story that really does transcend class."—*Eloisa James, New York Times bestselling author, on Tempt the Devil*

"*Seven Nights in A Rogue's Bed* is a lush, sensuous treat. I was enthralled from the first page to the last and still wanted more."—*Laura Lee Guhrke, New York Times bestselling author*

"No one does lovely, dark romance or lovely, dark heroes like Anna Campbell. I love her books."—*Sarah MacLean, New York Times bestselling author*

"It isn't just the sensuality she weaves into her story that makes Campbell a fan favorite, it's also her strong, three-dimensional characters, sharp dialogue and deft plotting. Campbell intuitively knows how to balance the key elements of the genre and give readers an irresistible, memorable read."—*RT Book Reviews, Top Pick, on Midnight's Wild Passion*

"Anna Campbell is an amazing, daring new voice in romance."—*Lorraine Heath, New York Times bestselling author*

"Ms. Campbell's gorgeous writing a true thing of beauty..."—*Joyfully Reviewed*

"She's the mistress of dark, sexy and brooding and takes us into the dens of iniquity with humor and class."—*Bookseller-Publisher Australia*

"Anna Campbell is a master at drawing a reader in from the very first page and keeping them captivated the whole book through. Ms. Campbell's books are all on my keeper shelf and *Midnight's Wild Passion* will join them proudly. *Midnight's Wild Passion* is a smoothly sensual delight that was a joy to read and I cannot wait to revisit Antonia and Nicholas's romance again."—*Joyfully Reviewed*

"Ms. Campbell gives us...the steamy sex scenes, a heroine whose backbone is pure steel and a stupendous tale of lust and love and you too cannot help but fall in love with this tantalizing novel."—*Coffee Time Romance*

"Anna Campbell offers us again, a lush, intimate, seductive read. I am in awe of the way she keeps the focus tight on the hero and heroine, almost achingly so. Nothing else really exists in this world, but the two main characters. Intimate, sensual story with a hero that will take your breath away."—*Historical Romance Books & More*

ALSO BY ANNA CAMPBELL

Claiming the Courtesan

Untouched

Tempt the Devil

Captive of Sin

My Reckless Surrender

Midnight's Wild Passion

The Sons of Sin series:
Seven Nights in a Rogue's Bed

Days of Rakes and Roses

A Rake's Midnight Kiss

What a Duke Dares

A Scoundrel by Moonlight

Three Proposals and a Scandal

The Dashing Widows:
The Seduction of Lord Stone

Tempting Mr. Townsend

Winning Lord West

Pursuing Lord Pascal

Charming Sir Charles

Catching Captain Nash

Lord Garson's Bride

The Lairds Most Likely:

The Laird's Willful Lass

The Laird's Christmas Kiss

The Highlander's Lost Lady

The Highlander's Defiant Captive

The Highlander's Christmas Quest

Christmas Stories:

The Winter Wife

Her Christmas Earl

A Pirate for Christmas

Mistletoe and the Major

A Match Made in Mistletoe

The Christmas Stranger

Other Books:

These Haunted Hearts

Stranded with the Scottish Earl

THE CHRISTMAS STRANGER

As the wayfarer traverses these isolated Yorkshire valleys, he is oftentimes struck by the lucky survival of diverse quaint fancies that the common folk persist in holding true. One charming legend from Fraedale in the High Pennines relates that a stranger's arrival during Advent signals a year of great good fortune ahead. Strangers being something of a rarity in these wild and remote corners of the realm, the good luck isn't as widespread as perhaps it might prove in gentler parts of the country. So a traveler at Christmas always receives a warm welcome, which given the generally inhospitable nature of the landscape, especially in the harsh winters, he may very well need.

— *Travels Through the Kingdom of Britain* (1787) by the Rev. Dr. Hector Chudleigh Quayle, M.A., D.D. (Oxon)

PROLOGUE

Jesus College, Oxford, 1ˢᵗ December 1821

As a highly respected expert on ancient Athenian politics, Dr. Thomas Black devoted the bulk of his time to reading.

However the letter holding his attention, as he sat at his desk amidst the dusty jumble of his college rooms, didn't date from the 5th century BC, but from last Thursday. Which was a pity. He'd much prefer to peruse a communication from a couple of thousand years ago.

What did he know of the modern world? And frankly, what did he care?

He sighed, not for the first time, and directed a longing glance at the thick report that had arrived this morning from Dr. Albert. Albert was a lucky dog, excavating in Greece for the entire winter. How Dr. Black itched to learn more of his colleague's recent discoveries.

But nobody could say that Thomas Black was completely lost to his duty.

Besides, he still harbored a soft spot for Kitty Hale. Even if he'd spent the last thirty years thanking his Maker that, when he and his best friend had pursued the lovely Miss Katherine Summers during that long ago London season, she'd chosen Cedric instead of him. He really wasn't cut out to be a husband.

Now Kitty wrote to embroil him in a family matter, wanting him to interfere in her son's life. Although Dr. Black supposed that given the young man in question was his godson, she had some right to enlist his assistance.

Once more, his eye fell on the offending lines.

Thomas, I'm at my wits' end, and I would dearly love your help if you're able to give it.

Joss is doing well in his career—you've probably heard of his success as an architect. Everyone in society is clamoring for him to rebuild their old houses in the fashionable gothic style.

Thomas vaguely recalled Kitty's letter last Christmas. There had been something in that about his godson making a splash in the world. Or at least he thought so. He always got the news about the children mixed up. With seven Hale offspring to sort out in his mind, a lot of Kitty's tattle went over his head. He hadn't seen any of the family in the last twenty years, although they always invited him to visit for the Festive Season.

He went back to reading the letter.

He needs to find a nice girl and settle down. He's approaching thirty and more than ready to move into the next stage of his life.

Dr. Black scowled at the paragraph. Reading between the lines, as a scholar was wont to do, those words implied that Kitty thought her former suitor, now a confirmed bachelor, was stuck in his childhood, too. What cheek.

But I've introduced him to every eligible girl in Sussex, and he won't have a bar of any of them. When he's in London, he just runs around with unsuitable women.

That raised a reminiscent smile. Dr. Black recalled the escapades of his youth well enough to understand the appeal of unsuitable women. He hadn't exactly been a devil for the ladies, but he hadn't been dead either.

Now I turn to you as his godfather. I realize you lead a retired life, but surely there's some charming girl you know, the daughter of a colleague or a relative, who might suit Joss.

He's got a good heart, although his manners aren't the most polished. And he's clever. So I need a girl outside the normal run. Which is one of the reasons I thought of you. I imagine Oxford is overflowing with clever women. All those fusty old dons you know must surely have a niece or a sister with brains.

Fusty old dons? He hoped she wasn't including him in that category.

Or perhaps someone you worked with in the early days ended up leaving college to marry and now has an attractive daughter. Can you think of a lady who won't bore Joss silly within the first ten minutes? If so, could you arrange for him to meet her?

One thing more—it would help if she was pretty. All the unsuitable women are diamonds of the first water. I suspect unsuitable women usually are. My son is not a shallow man —in fact, he's a bit of a romantic, and that's why he's so reluctant to commit himself. I believe he wants to fall in love. But I always think it's easier for a man to fall in love with a girl who isn't a complete antidote.

Kitty then revealed the iron hand under the velvet glove.

So far, your obligations as Joss's godfather have been far from onerous. And I'm persuaded your aid in assuring my son's future happiness won't demand much of your attention.

"Are you just, Kitty, my girl?" he asked aloud, breaking the untidy room's silence.

As if smart, pretty girls seeking a rough brute of a bridegroom grew on trees. Dr. Black wasn't remotely deceived by that line about "unpolished manners." If his doting mother described him thus, the boy must behave like a navvy in company.

Without much optimism, his mind winnowed through the few unmarried girls he knew. If they were pretty, they were silly. If they weren't silly, they weren't pretty. Young women were as much of a mystery as the vagaries of the world outside the walls of his cozy college. He inhabited an almost entirely masculine environment.

Dr. Black drew a sheet of paper forward and picked up his pen to begin a letter. He'd inform Kitty that she could harp on about his obligations to her second son all she liked, but Thomas Black could be of no assistance in this matter.

Then he paused and frowned thoughtfully into the distance.

Now he considered further, that wasn't quite true. He might just have a girl in mind.

Kitty Hale wanted her son to find a wife out of the common way? Dr. Black knew someone who fitted that description, both literally and figuratively. Further, Black had long ago decided to do something for the chit. Settle money on her. Find her a suitable situation. Put her in the care of someone who could help her make her way. Arrange a husband. That sort of thing.

He well remembered seeing the girl at her mother's funeral and planning to fix her up in life.

Had that really been a year ago?

Unfamiliar guilt stabbed him as he frowned down at the empty page in front of him.

By heaven, that wasn't a year ago. No, it had been five years.

All this time, Miss Margaret Carr had been stagnating up in Yorkshire. Dr. Black didn't make a habit of dwelling on his personal failings, but even he admitted he'd been deplorably careless about his orphaned cousin.

He'd meant to place the girl somewhere fitting to her rank. How unforgivable that he'd retreated into his selfish concerns and completely forgotten her, despite paying her a wage and providing a roof over her head.

She was pretty, very much so, and she was unusual —and her father, the vicar, had been a dashed clever fellow. With luck, her papa had passed his brains on to his only offspring. Perhaps she was precisely the woman to satisfy both Kitty and her wayward son.

It would take strategy to get Joss and Margaret together. Even Dr. Black knew enough about worldly young men to see that once they caught the slightest whiff of manipulation, they ran for the hills. Which was obviously where Kitty was going wrong with all her local belles.

He lifted his pen once more, but paused before writing. Was this wise, what he plotted? Joss Hale sounded like a bit of a lad. One mustn't discount all those unsuitable London ladies. What if the boy was an out-and-out libertine?

But there were other servants in the house in Yorkshire. Dr. Black was almost sure he paid more than one set of wages every month as a standing order from his bank. Margaret would have plenty of chaperones to keep her safe from a seducer's wiles.

Anyway, it was well past time Joss saw the estate up there. After all, it was to come to him in the end—not that Dr. Black wanted to tempt fate by telling the boy that.

Pleased with this easy solution to two problems, Joss's bride and Margaret's future, he started to write.

Dear Joss,

Forgive me for being such a neglectful godparent and for writing to you out of the blue like this. But I find myself in need of an architect to visit Thorncroft Hall in Fraedale in Yorkshire, with a view to undertaking largescale modernization.

I'd very much appreciate it if you could travel up there at your earliest convenience and report on the state of the building and what work needs to be undertaken to bring the old place up to date.

If you feel able to assist me in this, I'll be most grateful. In the hope that you're amenable to my request, I'm attaching details of the location. The house is ready for guests, and I'll let the servants know to expect you.

Yours affectionately,

Thos. Black

Now he must write to Margaret and tell her to prepare for a visitor. Then he'd answer Kitty's letter and share his dashed brilliant plan. He was a capital canny fellow, even if he did say so himself. Fusty old dons came in very handy sometimes, damn Kitty's impudence and fine green eyes.

He'd write that letter to Yorkshire. And the letter to Sussex. Of course he would.

Just as soon as he opened Dr. Albert's report. One little peek before he got back to his correspondence. His colleague's last letter had finished in a most suspenseful manner, after the discovery of a cache of stone tablets.

With a decisive gesture, Dr. Black sealed the letter to Joss and rose to put it on the table near the door, ready for his scout to collect and post this evening.

One glance to see what the report contained, then he'd write the other letters. He tore open the package from Dr. Albert and settled back at his desk, immediately engrossed in an ancient world that seemed so much more alive to him than the trivial matters filling the present.

The late autumn day closed in, and it was time to go to hall for dinner. Dr. Black's longsuffering scout collected the first letter, but there were no letters to follow.

Dr. Black disappeared back into his concerns and never answered Kitty's letter or wrote to Thorncroft Hall to let Margaret know company was on the way.

CHAPTER ONE

Thorncroft Hall, Fraedale, Yorkshire, 19th December 1821

"I hate to leave you on your own, Maggie. And at Christmas, too."

Maggie Carr mustered a smile for her friend and colleague Jane Parker. They'd been through this a hundred times already. She passed Jane her bag and opened the massive door leading out from the hall to the drive.

"Jane, your daughter's baby is due. Your place is in Goathland with the family."

"But you'll be all alone. What if someone comes?"

"Nobody's going to come. Nobody ever does."

Her employer, an eccentric and aging Oxford don, never traveled north to visit his small manor house in this isolated valley. And there were no passing travelers. They were miles away from a main route.

Jane must have picked up the wistful note Maggie tried so hard to suppress. With a decisive bang, she put down her bag. Her lined face set in a mulish expression. "That's it, then. I'm not leaving you alone in this great barn of a place. You're coming with me."

Maggie summoned another smile and picked up the bag. "You know your daughter's cottage will be bulging at the seams with you there, as well as her husband and the other two children. You're lovely to worry about me, Jane. But I'll be fine here. I've been on my own before."

"But not at Christmas." Jane looked torn. "How I wish you had some family to go to."

So did she. But she'd long ago learned the futility of wishes.

"I can't leave the house. You know Dr. Black wants someone in residence all the time." It was one of her employer's few demands.

"I'd feel better if Welby was here."

Welby was the outdoor man who looked after the garden and the pony, and did the heavy work in the house. In the depths of winter, with only two women living in, there was little for him to do.

"He'll come if there's an emergency."

"If he knows about it."

"He's only five miles away." Welby always spent December with his family in Little Flitwick, the nearest village. A wry smile twisted Maggie's lips. "And it's not like he's marvelous company."

If Welby spoke ten words a year, she'd be surprised. Jane, on the other hand, was a great talker. Maggie often wondered why the warmhearted woman had taken this situation such a long way from society. Although the pay was good and the work light. And Jane had a large family in the county who made sure she visited regularly.

Lucky Jane.

"Are you coming, missus?" the wagoner called from outside. "There be snow on the way, and I got other folk to collect."

"Snow on the way? Maggie, you can't stay here."

Maggie shook her head fondly and bundled Jane out of the door. "There's plenty of wood and food. If the snow traps me here, I'll just miss the Christmas service in the village. I'm sure God won't mind."

"Missus?"

Jane dithered for another second, before she bent to kiss Maggie's cheek. "Happy Christmas, then. Though I can't be easy about leaving you."

"I'll write."

Jane looked worried again. "If the mail makes it through the snow."

"Happy Christmas, Jane," Maggie said quickly, before Jane could yet again change her mind about going. "I'll see you in January."

The wagoner tossed the bag on board. Maggie hid a

smile as he struggled to get the plump and not terribly spry Jane up onto the wooden bench.

"Happy Christmas, Maggie," Jane called, as the driver urged his horse forward.

"And happy New Year, dear Jane," Maggie called back.

She stood on the doorstep until the wagon rolled out of sight. The heavy silence settled around her. Silence and solitude. Despite her brave words to Jane, she hated being alone at this time of year, when memories of her happy life with her parents returned to haunt her.

Once Christmas had been a joyous celebration of hope. Once she'd had a family. Once she'd had people who loved her. But no more.

With a sigh, she closed the door with a thud that she tried not to find ominous. She squared her shoulders and told herself to stop being so poor spirited. Things could definitely be worse.

Her father had been an impecunious clergyman, but the family had led a good life, if not a particularly luxurious one. Maggie hadn't known hardship until after he'd drowned, when she and her mother had to leave the Kentish vicarage that was the only home she'd ever known. Luckily her mother's cousin Thomas Black had offered the widowed Mrs. Carr a position as housekeeper at his Yorkshire estate. He'd given Maggie a home as well.

At the time, she'd been thinking of seeking a post as

a governess or companion, but after the tragedy of losing her father, the chance to stay with her mother was too appealing. Following her mother's death five years ago, she'd stayed on as housekeeper, although at twenty, she was really too young to take on the role. She'd been too heartsick with grief to think of setting up an independent life elsewhere. At least Thorncroft held memories of her mother.

Since then, she'd made a home of sorts here. She liked Jane and the taciturn Mr. Welby. And as housekeeper, she had more independence than any governess could aspire to.

But those few compensations offered frail cheer against spending the next weeks all alone, while the rest of the world celebrated Christmas.

In the years she'd been on her own, Maggie had done her best to stay brave and dutiful and faithful, as her beloved father had raised her to be. But there were times, like now, with the quiet house stretching around her, empty and echoing, when she could weep with loneliness.

"No use feeling sorry for yourself, my girl," she whispered.

She wished she hadn't spoken aloud. The sound reminded her that she wouldn't hear another human voice until after Twelfth Night.

Bitter experience had taught her that activity was the best answer to a case of the megrims. Bessie the cow needed milking, and she had Bob the pony to feed and his stall to muck out. There was nothing like pitching filthy straw to stop a person from brooding on what couldn't be changed.

But as Maggie trudged downstairs to the kitchens to put on her leather apron and work boots, she couldn't shake the grim feeling that life was passing her by. Unless some miracle took place, her youth would be gone, and she'd be old and alone, with nothing to show for the years.

Maggie stirred from sleep to a loud knocking downstairs. It was pitch dark, and she was on her feet and flinging a paisley shawl around her good thick flannel nightgown before she had time to think that it might be someone intending harm.

The knocking continued. She paused to light her candle from the embers of the fire, then picked up the poker. She'd have to see who it was. The snow had started soon after Jane left, and by the time Maggie dragged herself up to bed, it had become a full-blown storm. A traveler could be stranded. It was the code of the countryside that you helped strangers in need.

Still, she gripped the poker firmly as she made her way down the old oak staircase to the cavernous hall. She'd thought her room was cold, until she left it for the unheated vastness of the rest of the house. Shivering, she wished she'd paused to change into her merino gown and good stout half-boots.

She set her candle down on a carved chest. Down here, the knocking was deafening. It stopped when she pulled the heavy iron bolt back with a scrape. She turned the key and opened the door, battling to hold it against the howling wind.

"Who is it?" she asked, then gasped and faltered back when a powerful figure loomed up on the doorstep in front of her.

"Is this Thorncroft Hall?" a rough male voice barked.

The unknown man raised his lantern. His snow-covered hat was set low and shadowed his features. As fear tightened her stomach, Maggie began to wish she'd stayed in bed and ignored the knocking. Whoever the intruder was, he looked like a complete villain.

"Yes, it is." Although she raised the poker in silent warning.

It proved no deterrent. As he barged inside in a flurry of blown snow, he shot her weapon a contemptuous glance. "Just what do you intend to do with that, madam?"

"It's… Oh, blast." Her candle wasn't proof against the wind and went out. His lantern now provided the only light. "Don't imagine I'm defenseless."

The noise of the storm ceased abruptly as he seized the door from her and slammed it shut. "I'm pleased to hear it."

She tightened her grip on the poker and fought not to show her fear. "Kindly state your business, sir, or be gone."

"I don't respond to threats, miss," he said roughly. One massive hand reached over and plucked the poker from her as easily as if it was a dead twig on a tree.

"I'll scream," she said sharply, hoping he'd think the house was packed with burly footmen ready to come to her aid.

His lips flattened. "Scream away, for all the good it will do. I mean no harm."

The claim didn't reassure her at all. "So you say."

"So I say." With a faint sneer, he contemplated the poker in his powerful fist. "If a slip of a girl expects to frighten any self-respecting burglar with this, she's a complete nitwit."

Maggie sucked in a breath and for the first time, found that irritation outweighed fear. Her instincts told her that the intruder was too talkative to harbor evil intentions. And so far, he showed no propensity to violence, apart from stealing her poker.

"It was merely a precaution," she said stiffly.

"A waste of time, you mean."

How she wished she'd biffed this outspoken lout when she had the chance. Humiliated color heated her cheeks. That was the only warmth in the room. The hall was icy. "Have you come for any purpose, other than to be rude, sir?"

Unexpected amusement lifted the corners of his

mouth. "You took me by surprise when you answered the door in such dishabille."

She took him by surprise? That was rich. "I came down in a hurry, because I was worried that someone might be in trouble."

His wry smile shouldn't ease her fears. After all, there was no rule saying thieves and assassins must take life seriously.

He reached over to set the poker on top of the chest near her candle. Relinquishing the weapon was another good sign.

All right, perhaps this burly visitor wasn't about to knock her on the head and ransack the house.

"While I assumed you'd know who I am."

"I don't have that pleasure," she said sarcastically.

"I'm Joss Hale."

The name was clearly supposed to mean something to her. She drew in a deep breath and struggled to sound polite. Joss Hale mightn't be a bandit, but he was still an unmannerly toad. "Are you lost, Mr. Hale?"

"No." He raised his lantern and subjected her to a thorough survey. Something about his interest as he took in the sight of her made her wrap her shawl more securely around herself. Maybe he wasn't here to steal the silver, but theft wasn't the only crime a man could commit.

Her chilled fingers flexed with the urge to grab the poker once more. Not that she had a prayer of keeping him at bay. He was the size of Ben Nevis and just as thickly covered in snow.

"Are you injured?"

"No."

She bit back an annoyed exclamation. It was too cold to stand about playing silly questions. "Then what are you doing here?"

Vaguely she was aware that she wasn't acting like a servant, but he'd given her a nasty scare. She might have decided he wasn't about to murder her, but she was still badly rattled. And dear heaven, how she wished he'd stop staring at her.

"I'm expected. And why the devil you couldn't leave some lights on for me, I can't fathom. I only found this blasted house through sheer luck."

She bit back a protest at the bad language and frowned. "Expected?"

"Yes." He set the lantern on the chest and took off his hat, releasing a gust of snow onto the flagstones. His black greatcoat was also covered in white. "Pray send for the housekeeper, Mrs. Carr. She'll know all about it."

Before her abrupt awakening, Maggie had been dreaming about her parents. Now hearing this oaf mention her mother made her wince. "Mrs. Carr is my mother."

"I'm delighted to hear it." Impatience thinned the man's mouth, long and firm above a rock-like jaw shadowed with black whiskers. "So can you fetch her?"

"She's been dead five years." Maggie was too on edge to soften the stark words.

The man looked startled. "I was told to ask for her."

"I'm Miss Carr."

"You'll have to do, then." He didn't sound pleased. Too bad. He wasn't the one whose feet were freezing on icy flagstones. She rubbed one foot over another in an attempt to restore circulation. Her toes ached with cold. "Have a man look after my horse, and I'd like a brandy and some hot food in a room that isn't like a bloody ice cave. Perhaps you could get a footman to lay a fire in the library or drawing room."

Who on earth was this demanding brute? Maggie tightened her grip on her shawl, wishing she'd coshed him with the poker, instead of letting him into the house. Not that she'd invited him. He'd pushed his way in, without a by-your-leave.

She drew herself up to her full height. Unfortunately, she was only five feet five, while the stranger must be at least six foot three. The ice she injected into her voice was colder than the air around her. She ignored a whisper at the back of her mind, warning her that if he knew the name of the house and its housekeeper, he might indeed have a right to be here.

"Mr. Hale, before you take over the whole place, would you care to explain what you're doing here?"

His eyes, dark and deep-set, so in the uncertain light she couldn't make out their exact color, sharpened on her. "Good God, girl, you're freezing."

Her lips tightened. "Mr. Hale—"

He scowled at her from under thick black brows. "Go upstairs and put on something warm at once."

"You have no right to give orders, sir," she snapped. "As if I'd let a stranger roam about the house without supervision."

He released a longsuffering sigh. "And while you're supervising me, you're turning a fetching shade of blue."

"What color I turn is none of your concern." She winced at how childish she sounded.

"I give you my word, my purposes are honest."

"And how am I to know that, other than you telling me so?"

"Oh, for pity's sake. God save me from obstinate women." He reached forward and grabbed her by the waist, flinging her over one brawny shoulder. She landed on her stomach, punching the breath from her lungs. "Where's the nearest fire? You'll catch your death, if I don't take you somewhere warm."

Pounding on his back was like beating at the mountain he so resembled. "Put me down!"

She kicked him, but in this undignified position, it was difficult to gain momentum. He caught up the lantern and laid one powerful arm across her thighs, further restricting her movements.

"Where are the kitchens? I assume you've got a fire there."

"I'll have you up on a charge," she spluttered, as he moved along the corridor.

"Never mind. I'll find them myself. I'm an architect, and any architect worth his salt can find the kitchens."

"I insist you put me down," she said breathlessly, as he started descending the stairs.

Oh, dear, this was rather disorienting. She closed her eyes and ignoring the dictates of pride, clung to the back of his thick wool coat, damp with melting snow. Although how snow could melt in this temperature, she had no idea.

"Stop your griping, woman." He swung around the landing, making her stomach dip. "Where in blazes are the servants?"

Heavens above, was it safe to admit she was alone? She was too shocked and angry to be frightened. Which was stupid. If ever a man had proven himself her physical superior, this one had.

Perhaps she was wrong about him not being a murderer, and he was carting her downstairs to kill her. Except if murder was his intention, there was nobody and nothing to stop him murdering her upstairs. And it would save him the trouble of hauling her around.

Not that her weight seemed to inconvenience him. He wasn't even breathing unsteadily.

"Miss Carr?" Juggling the lantern, he pushed at the door to the kitchens. The wavering light increased her queasiness, so she was very glad when he strode across and deposited her in front of the banked hearth. She only just grabbed her shawl as she struggled to find her feet, although any protection it offered was purely token.

Maggie drew in a breath to tear strips off him, except the immediate warmth on her skin was too delicious. Her frozen toes curled into the rag rug and as he stoked up the fire, she felt a glorious heat on the back of her legs.

"You have no right to manhandle me," she said, wishing she sounded as outraged as she should. Smith, the cat, raised her head from the oak settle in the corner, and cast Maggie a disapproving look.

"I had to do something." In a couple of strides, Mr. Hale set the lantern on the table and crossed the floor to close the door. He was so huge, he seemed to take up half the room. "You were just going to stand up there, wittering on and turning into an icicle."

Wittering on? The nerve of the man. "If you introduced yourself like a gentleman, I might have felt up to inviting you in."

He stomped back to stand in front of her. That strange light in his eyes persisted. Odd that it warmed her even more effectively than the fire behind her. "You can't blame me for my lack of polite address. I was taken aback to find myself greeted by a wood sprite in a nightdress, instead of a respectable housekeeper."

"I'm respectable." She pushed aside a faint pleasure at the romantic description. It was too late for him to dredge up whatever shreds of rusty charm he might possess. "You're the one who needs to establish his credentials."

His scowl was truly fearsome. "You mean you really are the housekeeper?"

How she wished she'd waited to put on some clothes before she came downstairs. If he saw her in her dull gray gown, he'd have no trouble identifying her as a senior servant.

She raised her chin and shot him a quelling glare. That quelled him not at all. "I am, sir."

To her chagrin, he laughed. "You don't look old enough to be out on your own."

Her voice turned frostier. "Nevertheless, this house is under my care."

He shook his head in disgust. "Then why the devil wasn't someone waiting up for me? I know I'm later than I said I'd be, but when it started to snow, you must have expected that."

"I would have," she said with sweet sarcasm, "if I'd had a glimmer of a warning that you were coming. Are you sure it's this Thorncroft Hall you aim to infest?"

"You give as good as you get, don't you?" Appreciation was the last response she expected her insolence to garner. "Is there another Thorncroft Hall? And this is definitely the valley I want. Not that anyone else seems to want it. I haven't seen hide nor hair of another person for hours. It's like a lost world."

She didn't want him dwelling on their isolation.

Although she couldn't see how to stop him discovering that they were alone. Unless she could persuade him to leave in the next few minutes.

"There's a village about five miles further on," she said with a trace of desperation, although heavy snow always made the way impassable and it would be unchristian to force him back out into the night.

Mr. Hale gave a grunt of bleak humor. "My mistake. Fraedale's a bustling urban center, a veritable metropolis."

Far from it. "And there's an inn at Tolbeath another three miles from there."

"I don't want a damned inn. I want to stay here, as arranged with Thomas Black."

Oh, dear, if he knew Dr. Black owned this house, he must be in the right place. Her stomach sank, not least because if Dr. Black had invited Mr. Hale, she owed this interloper more courtesy than so far she'd managed to demonstrate. "Not with me."

"But Thomas Black has to be your employer. Although he doesn't strike me as a man to entrust a valuable property to a sprite barely out of the schoolroom."

"I'm twenty-five," she said, before she could stop herself.

As she should have expected, that didn't impress him. "Positively ancient."

"I'm old enough to run this establishment."

He looked around with a speaking expression.

"Place seems completely understaffed. Now roust someone out of bed to look after my horse, and get a maid to unearth some dinner. I haven't eaten since noon, and I've traveled a long and chilly way since then." As the tall clock in the hall upstairs chimed midnight, he started to take off his coat.

Maggie bit her lip. There was no point putting it off any longer. "Don't take off your coat, Mr. Hale."

He tilted a brow in her direction. "Miss Carr, I can prove my identity."

She made a defeated gesture. "I'm sure you can." He was too confident to be some random intruder. "But you'll need to go back outside to put your horse in the stable."

He was back to scowling again, those thick black brows lowering over his commanding beak of a nose. "What about the grooms?"

"There are no grooms. There are no maids," she said shakily. She tangled nervous fingers in the fringe of her shawl. "I'm completely on my own here."

CHAPTER TWO

*J*oss stared appalled at the exquisite creature with the willowy form and delicate, pointed face. This girl belonged in some enchanted realm, not in an empty house in a godforsaken valley. "What the devil do you mean, alone?"

No wonder she hadn't given him a warmer welcome. When he turned up on her doorstep, twice as large as life, he must have scared her out of her mind. Not that anyone would know it. She'd been as game as a terrier protecting her domain.

Guilt at his high-handed behavior pricked at him, although he couldn't entirely regret touching her. That part, he'd enjoyed, although he'd known even at the time that he shouldn't.

"You know what alone means." Pink edged the fairy's slanted cheekbones, and she cast him an annoyed look. The fairy didn't like him much.

And whose fault was that? He probably shouldn't have taken matters into his own hands, when it came to shifting her downstairs.

Probably? Definitely. But the girl had been ready to stand on that cold stone floor and quarrel with him, until she turned into a block of ice. Joss had just chosen the commonsense solution.

He gestured around the large and well-appointed room. "This is a blasted manor house."

"A small manor house."

"It's still too big to have only one wisp of a girl rattling around inside it. Won't Black pay to staff it?"

Miss Carr continued to regard Joss as if he was something nasty eating her daffodils. At least she no longer looked like she turned into an icicle. Although standing as she was in front of the fire, she presented a disturbing picture.

The nightgown wasn't designed to entice. In fact, he remembered Granny Hale wearing something very similar. But the effect of thick white flannel on Miss Carr was quite different, especially when the fire behind her was kind enough to reveal the shadowy shape of the body under the voluminous folds. The curves of waist and hip. The lissome line of her legs.

When he'd picked her up—something she wasn't likely to forgive for a century at least—he'd thought there was nothing to her. But the naughty firelight proved him wrong. She might be a mere morsel, but what was there was prime quality.

Joss realized she was talking, in that precise voice with its husky edge that did nothing to subdue his masculine urges. When he'd pushed his way into the house, he'd felt frozen to the bone. He didn't feel cold at all now. "What?"

That wasn't polite. She didn't have to tell him so. He was a lumbering bear of a man at the best of times. Faced with Miss Carr's ethereal perfection, he felt like he could out-Caliban Caliban.

Yet this vision proclaimed herself to be something as prosaic as a housekeeper.

The world was going mad.

She started speaking slowly, as though he was deficient in understanding. By God, she might be right.

He dragged his gaze from where the flannel draped across her hips and met her eyes. Sky blue. Striking, combined with the rich red hair tied into a thick plait that snaked over her shoulder and across her breast.

A round, luscious breast…

Damn it, not what he needed to think about. But he dared any man with blood in his veins to resist noticing.

That dratted swirly blue and red shawl covered her top half as effectively as modesty could wish. But that didn't stop him wondering about what lay underneath.

"With six bedrooms," she said sharply, breaking into his thoughts on whether her nipples were pink or brown. Right now, he leaned toward a lovely creamy brown, like lightly toasted toffee.

She must have been running through the details of the house. Luckily Uncle Thomas had enclosed a rough description of the manor with his letter, so Joss could sound as if he'd been listening, instead of picturing her naked.

"And usually there's another woman and an outdoor man to help."

"So where are they?" He struggled to comprehend that he and this fiery-haired sprite were alone together in the middle of this damned wilderness.

She sighed and for a brief instant, stopped looking like a pocket Boadicea. "Jane's daughter's about to have a baby, so she left this afternoon. In the middle of winter, Mr. Welby only comes up from the village if there's something urgent."

He frowned. "You're on your own for Christmas?"

She scowled, as though he'd accused her of purloining his pocket watch. Odd. He didn't see the question as particularly combative.

"I'm perfectly happy here."

The defensive note indicated that he'd hit a sore spot. "There's no need to fly up into the boughs. I'm on my own for Christmas, too." Then the full significance of what she'd said struck him. "Damn it, I was going to have Christmas here, but I can't now. In fact, I'll have to ride on. Five miles to the village, do you say? If you'll fix me something to eat before I go, I'll be on my way."

She looked startled and not very pleased at his announcement. Which seemed mighty contrary. Upstairs, she'd pretty much shown him the door. "Now what in Hades is wrong with you?"

"I do wish you'd mind your language, sir."

He scowled back. "Most people take me as they find me."

Her dismissive expression conveyed her opinion of that. She went back to speaking as if he was a beef-witted clodhopper. "You came here through a blizzard."

If he went back out into that white hell, his poor bloody horse would never speak to him again. He'd kept the mare going the last few arduous miles with promises of oats and a warm stable. "Believe me, I know."

She spread her hands so the shawl shifted in a promising way. All the moisture dried from his mouth, as he prayed the blasted thing would just vanish altogether. "You're lucky you got this far. This is dangerous country, Mr. Hale. People freeze to death in a Yorkshire winter."

He could imagine. And damn and blast, it turned out he'd got all excited over nothing. The shawl remained as stubbornly concealing as ever.

"You must see it's impossible for me to stay." He tried to sound gentle. It wasn't his natural mode, and he could see it didn't persuade Miss Carr.

"You're worried about the proprieties." She sounded like she didn't believe it. Given how he'd hoisted her over his shoulder a few minutes ago, he couldn't blame her.

"Indeed I am. The two of us shouldn't be alone together under one roof."

She regarded him as if he made no sense. "But I'm a servant."

A very insubordinate one, but he forbore to point that out. If he was going, he needed to go now. Much as he'd rather stay in this warm room, arguing with this truculent fairy. "A very pretty servant. Believe me, if the world finds out, it will pay attention."

She didn't seem to notice his compliment. He supposed she was used to men tumbling over themselves to tell her how lovely she was. The biggest puzzle of this puzzling situation was how the blazes this beguiling creature had managed to reach the advanced age of twenty-five while remaining *Miss* Carr.

Her laugh held a hint of grimness. "What world? This place is the back of beyond."

"Are you saying you want me to stay?"

"I'm saying that at least for tonight and probably a few days to come, you can't go anywhere else because the snow blocks the road over the hills. And even if you do get to Little Flitwick, there's no inn. You're in the wilds, Mr. Hale, not the middle of London."

"You tried to get me to go away before."

"I shouldn't have." She looked uncomfortable. "It's just—"

He sent her a straight look. "You were on your own, and there was a stranger outside."

She raised her chin. "Well, you're no longer a stranger. Or not entirely. And I don't want your death on my conscience."

He straightened with a sigh, although hearing her say he wasn't a stranger pleased him more than it should. Especially if he needed to keep his hands off her until the snow melted. "Then I'd better get my horse into the stable. At least for tonight. We can reassess in the morning."

"I'll help you."

"No, you damn…dashed well won't. One of us freezing his arse off is enough." Hmm, his attempt at controlling his language wasn't working too well. "Just tell me where to go."

To his surprise, her lips quirked. "I'm too much of a lady for that."

He gave a grunt of appreciative laughter. Had his sprite with eyes like the summer sky made a joke? He knew it was wrong to stay, but he couldn't stifle his anticipation at the thought of seeing more of her.

And he didn't just mean that slender, graceful body.

Maggie took advantage of Mr. Hale's absence to rush upstairs and dress like the housekeeper she was. Coming back to the kitchens, she stoked up the fire and started making him a meal. By the time he stomped back into the kitchens, she felt much more composed.

She was horribly aware how rude she'd been when Mr. Hale was here with her employer's approval. She put on her best housekeeper voice. "Do you mind eating down here, sir? It's the warmest room."

He cast her a doubtful frown as he set his saddlebags near the door. When he tugged off his hat and coat, he sent snow scattering across the stone floor. "You sound unusually polite."

"I hope you'll pardon me." She dipped into a curtsy. "I didn't treat you the way a guest to this house deserves to be treated."

The sardonic arch of his black brows made her want to clout him. Again. But she doubted if her hardest punch would make a dent.

She'd expected him to appear less formidable, once he'd removed the bulky greatcoat and high-crowned beaver hat. But if anything, he loomed even larger.

She paused to study him. Everything about him was big. His chest. His shoulders. His head with its unruly mop of coal-black curls. Large hands. Large feet. Long powerful legs displayed to advantage in buckskin breeches.

She blushed and glanced away. Those tight breeches did little to hide that his remarkable size was thanks to acres of hard muscle.

In comparison, she felt like a mere dot.

Mr. Hale wasn't a handsome man. At least in terms of the fashionable beaux sketched in the papers. And she couldn't imagine him featuring as the hero of a novel.

The villain, perhaps.

Maggie's experience of gentlemen her own age was limited, and Mr. Hale couldn't be more than thirty. She reluctantly admitted that, while he mightn't be conventionally good looking, he was attractive. Standing like a mountain in the middle of the floor, he vibrated with energy and intelligence. However appalling his manners, it was difficult to dislike him. It seemed she'd already forgiven him for hauling her around like a sack of potatoes.

"I must apologize for my earlier manner," she continued.

She had no idea why the glance he bestowed upon her plain—dowdy—gray dress held a hint of disappointment. "Must you?"

"Yes," she said stiffly.

Oh, dear, was that a note of challenge? When she caught that mocking glint in his eyes, something in her reacted like dry wood to a flame. She reminded herself of her humble status. And the fact that if Dr. Black threw her out on her ear for upsetting the first guest he'd invited to Thorncroft since her mother's funeral, she had nowhere else to go.

"I hate to play Devil's advocate, but I turned up in the middle of the night with no warning. I did write, but I suspect the bad weather further south has delayed my letter. I'm well aware that not even my best friend would call me anything but rough and ready."

She'd already worked out that Joss Hale was nobody's advocate. Although she was yet to be convinced that he wasn't the devil. A seducer of souls would have a voice like his. Deep to the point of subterranean, but rich with a velvety edge, when he wasn't marching about, throwing orders around.

Maggie struggled for the civil, uninvolved tone she'd decided to adopt with Mr. Hale. If he and she were to live under one roof, even for a short time, they had to preserve the gulf between master and servant. Given the interest she'd seen in his eyes earlier, she wanted him to think of her as a housekeeper, not a woman.

Then she remembered with horror what he'd said about spending Christmas at the house. With difficulty, she squashed her disquiet down until it formed a knot of seething disquiet in her stomach.

She had tonight to get through. Let tomorrow's troubles wait.

"Nevertheless, I greeted you in a totally inappropriate fashion. I'd like to start again." She curtsied once more and narrowed her eyes at him when his lips twitched.

"My name is Margaret Carr. I'm the housekeeper here at Thorncroft Hall. I'll do my best to make your stay comfortable."

He tilted his chin in the direction of the saucepan on the hob. "In that case, my soup is about to boil over."

"Oh, no." She whirled around and rescued the soup. She poured it into an earthenware bowl, hoping he didn't expect the best china at this hour. "Please sit down."

He took a seat, and she let out a relieved breath. It was nice to have him on the same level at last. "Will you join me?"

She shook her head. "No, thank you. I've eaten. Anyway—"

"You're about to say something housekeeperish, aren't you?"

She ignored the jibe and slid the steaming bowl in front of him, then a plate of bread and butter. Perhaps once he'd eaten, he'd be easier to handle. "Would you like wine or ale? Or there's brandy."

"Wine, please," he said, trying the steaming vegetable soup. The expression of pleasure on his face made him look younger and considerably more approachable. "By God, this is good. Did you make it?"

Stupid girl she was, she blushed with gratification. But it was nice to hear a compliment for her cooking from someone other than Jane.

"Thank you. Yes." Feeling more settled, now he was sitting down and focusing on his meal instead of her, she opened the bottle of Dr. Black's claret that she'd brought up from the cellar.

"Could you...could you tell me why you're here,

sir?" She poured him a glass. "Thorncroft isn't on the way to anywhere, and we rarely..." Never. "...get visitors."

"If word gets out about your cooking, that will change." He'd practically inhaled the soup. She couldn't doubt that he'd been hungry. Perhaps that explained his boorishness. As he drank some of his wine, she took his bowl and refilled it.

She almost felt in charity with her unwelcome guest, until he leaned back in his plain oak chair and set to watching her again. Her momentary ease disappeared, and she became painfully conscious that they were alone.

It was ridiculous, getting nervous now. They'd managed a polite exchange, and she was treating him like a servant should. Mostly.

"I thought I told you who I was," he said.

She busied herself making roast beef sandwiches to follow his soup, although under that considering dark gaze—she still wasn't sure what color his eyes were—her usually deft hands fumbled. Smith, smelling the meat, left her comfortable spot and began to twine around her legs.

"You told me your name."

He raised the half-full wineglass that dangled from one large hand and drank. "I wish you'd have some wine."

"Why? Is the news so bad that I need to be in my cups?"

His mouth curved upward. Most of him was huge and rugged and powerful. But that expressive mouth hinted at another side to him. An easier, more affable side.

It was a very nice mouth. Sharply cut and with a full lower lip. She'd never been kissed, but…

The knife slipped, luckily mangling the slice of beef, not her hand.

What in creation had her thinking of kisses?

"I don't think some wine will hurt." He reached over to catch her hand, making her start. "And you've already cut enough meat to feed an army. I know I'm a big cove, but…"

His hand was cool on hers. So why did his touch send heat rushing through her?

"I'll sit," she croaked, shifting away. Smith, disappointed at not cadging a treat, strutted back to the rug in front of the fire.

To Maggie's surprise, Mr. Hale rose and pulled out a chair for her. Then he turned and fetched another glass from the sideboard. She wanted to insist that such courtesy was inappropriate, but the touch of his hand had stolen all her words. How he'd chortle if he knew that.

He sat down to finish his soup and take a last bite of bread with a snap of straight white teeth. While he ate, he studied her under lowered black brows. This seemed to be a characteristic expression.

She was glad she'd taken the time to light a couple

of lamps and stoke up the fire. The near darkness before had created an atmosphere that was much too intimate. What they both needed was a strong dose of the mundane. He poured her a glass of wine, ignoring her when she indicated that he should stop after a few drops.

He reached into his black jacket and withdrew a creased letter which he passed to her. "This is my most recent correspondence with Dr. Black. You'll see he asked me to come here. I'm an architect."

She remembered Mr. Hale muttering something along those lines when he dragged her downstairs. She'd been too furious to pay much attention. "An architect?"

He burst out laughing at her doubtful tone. "It's true."

She wasn't sure what she'd expected him to do for a living. A soldier of fortune, perhaps. A strongman in a fair. A Bow Street runner.

Architect seemed too…civilized.

Not to mention architects catered to clients who made demands and expected a modicum of deference, when she'd already discovered that Mr. Hale was a man with his own way of doing things.

He went on. "You're thinking I'm too rude to be an architect."

"A successful one at least," she blurted out, then blushed like fire. She wasn't proving much more cour-teous than Mr. Hale.

He smiled at her, and her heart stumbled to a quivering stop. Astonishment held her transfixed.

Dear Lord, had she grudgingly conceded that he was attractive? She'd had no idea. When he smiled, the bear-like aspect disappeared, and his face creased into vivid charm.

Her fingers tightened on the untouched glass of wine. Heaven help her, maybe she should send him on his way tonight, however likely he was to stumble into a snowy ditch and perish from the cold.

"You'd be wrong, Miss Carr," he went on, as if her world hadn't changed in an instant with a man's smile. "My brusqueness does my practice no harm at all. I have a well-earned reputation as a temperamental genius. The upper crust are quite convinced it's de rigueur to have me stomping around their houses, shouting about improvements."

Actually she could imagine he was good at his job, if not with his clients. Something about him suggested confidence and competence. And however much he looked like a prizefighter, there was the evidence of that mouth and those adept hands to indicate there was more to him than brute force.

She didn't look at the letter. "But what are you doing here? And why on earth is Dr. Black employing a fashionable architect? He never comes to Fraedale. I haven't seen him since my mother's funeral five years ago."

Mr. Hale shrugged. "Perhaps he wants to use the property more often. Perhaps he wants to sell."

Sell? That terrifying possibility sent every other thought fleeing from her mind.

"You've gone very quiet," Mr. Hale said in a worried tone.

There was no earthly reason he should care about what happened to her. They'd just met, and she'd hardly set out to endear herself. But as she set down the letter, she raised a troubled gaze to his face. "This is my home. I have nowhere else to go."

CHAPTER THREE

"Curse me for a clumsy blockhead," Joss said roughly, desperate to banish the desolation dulling Miss Carr's lovely blue eyes. "Please forgive me for speaking out of turn. I have no idea what my godfather intends. He didn't tell me. He just asked me to look at the house to see what alterations and repairs it needs."

"Your godfather?"

She sounded shaky, and he didn't like it. He liked it much better when she stood up to him. He nudged her wineglass toward her, and this time she did take a sip.

"He and my father went to Jesus College at Oxford together."

"Is your father still alive?"

"Yes, he and my mother live in Sussex."

She didn't look quite so lost anymore, thank God.

"What are you doing in wildest Yorkshire over Christmas? Don't you want to be with your family?"

Not when they plagued him every minute God sent about finding a wife. That was the problem with happily married couples. They wanted everyone else to be happily married, too.

Joss had long believed that he was too gruff and uncouth to arouse the matrimonial ambitions of any well-bred maiden. But it seemed the combination of an earl for an uncle, the fortune he'd inherited from a great-aunt, and his thriving, if unconventional architectural practice more than made up for the deficiencies in his manners. His mother had devoted the last two years to producing a stream of eligible girls, who turned up eager to impress him. So far, all the candidates had been suitable, pretty, and as dull as bad Palladian architecture.

He was sick to the stomach of chits who giggled and stammered and batted their eyelashes at him. Miss Carr had done none of those things yet. By Jove, perhaps if he got desperate, he should marry her.

"Now you've gone quiet," she said, sounding worried.

Joss summoned a smile and reached for the bread and meat she'd cut for him. "I've got six brothers and sisters, and a crowd of nieces and nephews. Nobody will miss me."

"But you might miss them," she said in a small voice.

Right now, looking at this pretty girl, he couldn't

imagine why he would. This pretty girl who seemed to have nobody in the world to care for her.

Curiosity ate at him. How had this jewel of a woman ended up here, hidden away from the world?

While he was perfectly prepared to break social rules and ask intrusive questions, he wasn't ready to keep her up when she looked so tired and drawn. And distressed.

How he regretted mentioning that Uncle Thomas might sell the house. Perhaps his godfather wanted to turn this isolated pile into an example of the fashionable gothic purely for his own pleasure.

But Thomas Black rarely left Oxford, and never unless he absolutely had to. During his years in business, Joss had developed a sixth sense about his clients and their intentions. Something in his godfather's letter hinted that his sudden decision to renovate his neglected property indicated an ending of some kind.

"Oh, I shouldn't be sitting here like this." She jumped to her feet and began to clear the table. "Let me show you to your room, sir."

Miss Carr seemed determined to treat him as her better, when he suspected she was his social equal in everything but fortune. She certainly sounded like his social equal, with that low, precise voice. "Don't you think we've progressed beyond sir?"

She picked up the meat dish and stubbornly shook her head. "Not at all, sir."

"And there's no need to make me up a room at this

hour. If I put two chairs together, I can sleep in here. It's nice and warm, and the cat can keep me company."

Again she shook her head, this time so emphatically that a couple of tendrils of rich red hair escaped from her ferociously tight coiffure. While he stabled Emilia, she'd pinned that thick plait up behind her head, and the dress she wore wouldn't disgrace a sixty-year-old dowager. Clearly she strove to convince him of her authority and maturity. A pity the plan backfired—she looked like a little girl wearing her mother's clothes.

For a moment, Joss stared into the distance, trying to identify the poignant emotion squeezing his heart. The best description he could manage was tenderness. Unfamiliar in his twenty-nine years, although he loved his family, no matter how annoying they could be.

The thought of facing life without them cut him like a blade.

Whereas Miss Carr didn't seem to have any family at all. In fact, she seemed more alone than anyone he'd ever met.

But Joss already knew her well enough to predict that she'd never forgive him if he said he felt sorry for her.

How wrong he'd been to imagine hundreds of beaux trailing after her. Her beauty seemed completely —and inexplicably—undiscovered. Which was a crying shame.

Unless you were the man who discovered her.

She tossed a scrap of meat to the large black and

white cat curling around her ankles, then placed the uneaten sandwiches on a plate. "Dr. Black insists that the house is always ready for visitors. There's a nice room at the top of the stairs."

"You said nobody ever comes."

"But someone might." She cast him an unreadable glance from those extraordinary azure eyes. "After all, you did."

Yes, he did. And felt like the luckiest cove in creation that he had. He'd cursed the snow all day, especially over the last few miles when he'd had his doubts that he'd reach shelter before he froze. Right now, in Miss Carr's company, the bad weather seemed like a blessing.

Perhaps his thoughts tended in such a curious direction because of the late hour. Not long ago, the clock upstairs had struck two.

Or because of the strange otherworldly atmosphere of this isolated house.

Or the woman. The lovely, intriguing woman.

But right now Joss felt like an enchanted prince caught up in a fairytale.

And because everyday rules didn't apply, he reached out to catch Miss Carr's wrist. She started under his touch. Fear? Or was she as vibrantly aware of him as he was vibrantly aware of her?

God only knew. And after the day he'd had, Joss was too tired to come up with an answer.

"It's late, Margaret. Why don't you go to bed? I can look after myself from here."

She studied him without shifting away. He waited for her to pull free, to insist that she was paid to serve, that he shouldn't call her Margaret, that she had to set the table or light the fire or shovel the snow.

"Finish your wine, sir." Her husky voice stroked across his skin like a caress. "When you go upstairs, your room is the first door to the right, along the corridor."

"Good night," he said softly, wishing she was giving him directions to her room, while recognizing that even if she did, no man of honor could take such brazen advantage of this situation.

With a slowness that set his heart crashing against his ribs, she withdrew from his hold. Avoiding his eyes, she curtsied and left him to the silent kitchens.

When Joss woke in the ancient four-poster in the pleasant, if old-fashioned bedroom, he wondered if he'd dreamed the events of last night, and he was back in his rooms at the Albany. Or perhaps in one of the inns he'd stayed in on his leisurely journey up from London. He'd taken the opportunity to view various big houses on his way. His godfather hadn't given him a date for reporting back on Thorncroft, so he hadn't hurried north.

Although if he'd known what awaited him here, he wouldn't have dallied.

Because of course he hadn't dreamed the night's events. A fact underlined when he shifted to sit on the edge of the mattress and every muscle protested. That long struggle through the blizzard left him feeling like he'd gone ten rounds with Gentleman Jackson.

The room was cold, and he stoked up the fire before he opened the heavy brown velvet curtains. A stark white world greeted him. The snowfall persisted.

Honor might dictate he moved on this morning, but common sense, not to mention self-preservation, would win that argument.

By the time he'd washed and shaved and dressed, he felt slightly less like something the cat had dragged in. He was hungry and wanted coffee. More, he wanted to see the girl from last night and discover if he'd imagined her devastating impact on his senses.

Not that he could do much about wanting her.

He'd enjoyed his fair share of women, and his fair share of women had enjoyed him. But they'd all known the game. None had been well-born virgins. Or servants who relied on a good reputation to keep their livelihoods.

Worse, Margaret, for all her spirit, was poor and defenseless and friendless. Only a cad of the worst kind would contemplate her seduction.

He was contemplating, all right. But he had no

intention of carrying through with his wicked thoughts.

Damn it.

Once the weather permitted, he'd ride on. He could come back after Christmas, once there was a chaperone or two in residence.

But, Lord above, how he relished the thought of having her to himself for the next few days.

Sighing and running his hand through his freshly combed hair, doubtless turning it into the usual bird's nest, he went downstairs.

In the pale light of day, he'd expected the fairytale atmosphere to evaporate. But as he wandered the rooms, the house was eerily silent. He wasn't a fanciful man, but it felt like Thorncroft's ghosts held their breath and watched, waiting to see what happened next.

Joss struggled to break free of the entangling coils of fantasy. He'd worked on ancient buildings before. They always cast a spell, especially these lovely Jacobean houses, that spoke so eloquently of an earlier age. But even as the architect in him noted fine linenfold paneling in the dining room, some pretty plasterwork in the drawing room, and the intricate carving on the main staircase, he felt like he stepped deeper and deeper into magic.

The house felt like an empty stage set. The leading lady was yet to appear.

In this enchanted realm, Christmas held no dominion. Joss found not a trace of greenery or decoration anywhere.

Down in the kitchens, a good fire blazed in the hearth, and he could smell baking bread. There was also, praise the angels, a pot of coffee. He paused to gulp some down, before he continued his search for Margaret.

As he drank, he glanced around, curious to discover clues about the woman who shared the house with him. He wasn't particularly careful of his appearance or his manners, but when it came to his work, he was organized and fastidious. So he appreciated this room's air of good management. And if that soup last night was any indication, she was a marvelous cook.

The black and white cat rose from the rug before the fire, stretched, and wandered over for some attention.

"Where's your mistress, puss?" Joss asked, scratching her behind the ears.

The cat butted his ankle with her head, before meandering outside. Joss was familiar enough with the rules of fairytales to know he should follow. He paused to throw on his greatcoat, left to dry in front of the fire, thanks to Margaret.

The cat strutted across the yard he remembered crossing last night. Today's gentle snow made it a much more appealing space than it had been in the howling blizzard.

When the cat disappeared into the stables, he

followed. Even if he didn't find Margaret there, he wanted to check on his horse. Emilia had been limping by the time they reached Thorncroft Hall, and he was worried about her.

As he entered the stable, Joss found his elusive fairy. She was walking away from him, carrying two full buckets. He gave into the ungentlemanly impulse to admire the fine view from the back.

She'd tucked her skirts up to reveal a pair of trim ankles in black stockings and wooden pattens. As she carried her load, her hips swayed from side to side with a rhythm that made his blood pound. The thick red hair was pinned up once more, but soft tendrils clung to her nape. For a sizzling instant, he stared at that pale skin at the back of her neck, and the urge to sink his teeth into her was so sharp, he could almost taste her.

He stepped forward. "Miss Carr?"

She stopped and turned, setting her buckets on the ground with a clink. They were full of water. "Mr. Hale, I thought you might sleep in. I'm just getting your horse some fresh water."

Her nervous tone hinted that she'd *hoped* he would sleep in. She hadn't sounded nervous last night. The implications of sharing the house with a man must be preying on her mind this morning.

"Let me." He expected her to argue, but she stepped aside meekly enough and let him collect the buckets.

"Thank you."

The day was cloudy, and through the high windows,

stark gray light shone on her face. It revealed details he'd missed last night. A sprinkle of delightful freckles across her straight little nose. Gold-tipped lashes shadowing those remarkable eyes. She still looked like a visitor from another world.

"I hope you slept after you left me," he said.

"Like a baby."

He had a feeling she was lying. "I'm glad."

On the other hand, he'd crashed into a slumber deeper than anything he'd recently enjoyed in London. He loved his work, but over the last year, a strange restlessness had possessed him. The days passed in their usual busy whirl, but he was aware of a lurking dissatisfaction that grew with every success. Ridiculous at twenty-nine to feel like he'd climbed all the mountains, but he definitely needed some new challenge.

His family would say he was discontented because he needed a wife. Devil take them.

Margaret bent to scratch the cat's ears. "How are you this morning, Smith?"

"Smith?"

"When my mother was a girl, Miss Smith was her governess."

A governess? He was right about Margaret being born to higher things than housekeeping. "Did she like her governess?"

"Oh, yes. She liked the cat, too."

The stables were warmer than outside. Marginally. The only other occupants, apart from his mare, were a stocky piebald pony and a Jersey cow that Margaret had already fed and watered, if the animal's contented munching was any indication. He gave the first bucket to the pony, then entered his horse's stall. As he filled her water trough, Emilia nickered in welcome and nudged him with her noble head.

"Hello, my old darling." He rubbed her nose and let the familiar scents of animals and hay and leather soothe his senses. "I hope you're feeling a bit more like yourself this morning."

Last night, poor Emilia had been completely beaten down and hadn't shown much interest in the oats he'd found for her. Now he patted her chestnut flank and noticed Margaret had replenished her manger. "There's no need for you to look after my horse."

Margaret came and leaned on the door. "I think she might be lame. She's favoring her right foreleg."

"Blast," he muttered, going down on his haunches to check. He immediately saw the swollen fetlock. No wonder Emilia had been limping. "I led her the last few miles to save her carrying me, but it mustn't have helped."

"You faced that blizzard on foot?"

He shrugged and began to run his hands down his mare's legs. Only the front one was in trouble. Not good news, but it could be worse. "Needs must."

"You won't be going anywhere today."

Unable to fathom Margaret's tone, he lifted his head

to study her—no great chore. "I could take your pony and go to the village."

She shook her head. "He's too old to deal with the snowdrifts. And there's more snow on the way."

He didn't bother questioning her statement. She'd lived here long enough to know the weather. "No trips to Little Flitwick?"

"You're stuck here until the weather improves."

Hurrah. "And when is that likely to be?"

Her lips twisted. "May."

He released a grunt of laughter as he stood. "I'll see what I can do with Emilia."

"Emilia?"

"I bought her in Emilia Romagna when I was on my grand tour. She's served me well since."

"Italy?" she breathed as if he'd offered her the key to heaven. He realized with no great surprise that this restricted life chafed at Margaret.

She was young and vital and beautiful. Of course it did.

"I'll tell you about it, if you like."

Hell, if he had his wish, he'd transport her there in a flash. The thought of a carriage ride to view the Colosseum by moonlight was damnably appealing. Or gliding along the Grand Canal in a Venetian gondola. Or taking a private box at La Fenice. By God, he'd make sure she didn't see much of the opera there.

"Oh, I'd like that." She straightened away from the stall door, and her expression turned neutral. After last night, he wasn't surprised at the change in her manner. Every time their interactions broached on intimacy, she pulled back and acted like a servant. Never very convincingly.

"I'm sorry," she said in a prim little voice, as the cat slunk over to sit at her feet. "I'm getting above myself, sir."

He rolled his eyes, while forbidden pictures of her being anything but prim flooded his mind and made his blood surge. "There are only two of us here."

Her lips tightened. "I'm well aware of that, sir."

"So do you think you could forgo calling me sir, given nobody else is around to give you points for humility?"

"It's not suitable."

With difficulty, he prevented himself from rolling his eyes again. "My presence here isn't suitable. Nothing else counts."

"Sir—"

"I insist you don't call me sir. No good servant disobeys a blatant command."

The blue eyes flashed azure with annoyance. "As you wish, Mr. Hale."

He supposed it was better than sir, but not much. "And what shall I call you?"

"Miss Carr." Her voice held a nice snap. He liked seeing the pepper in her.

"No. Margaret, I think."

"I prefer Miss Carr."

"But I'm giving the orders."

"Aren't you just?" she muttered.

He bit back a smile. "You've got too much spirit to be a servant."

To his surprise, her lips turned down in self-disgust. "I know. It's probably a good thing nobody ever comes here. If Dr. Black sells the house, I don't know who else will employ me. I'm really too young for such a senior post. But I couldn't bear—"

"Taking something further down the pecking order?"

"Yes."

He was sorry he'd made her sad again. "Uncle Thomas never said he was selling the house."

"No. Perhaps I'm worried about nothing." She bent to pick up the cat and rubbed her cheek against the top of Smith's head. Joss had never been jealous of a feline before. "Anyway, it's not your problem."

"I'll feel responsible if you lose your situation."

"Oh, no. It's not your fault." She raised her chin and straightened her back. Every time she did that, he felt like she defied a world that had treated her very shabbily indeed. "I'm sure Dr. Black won't cast me out into the world with nowhere to go. After all, we're distantly related."

"Are you indeed?"

The news was unexpected. What in Hades was Uncle Thomas doing, making a relative a bloody housekeeper? He had plenty of blunt. Enough to give this girl a London season, at the very least.

"Yes, cousins of a sort. Mamma worked it out and told me." She was still mulling over her future as she cuddled the cat. Lucky Smith. "I suppose I could find a place as a governess."

Joss's doubtful glance made her bristle, justifying his misgivings about this plan.

"I've had a good education," she said, as if he'd offered some argument. "Papa was an Oxford man and taught me Latin and history and mathematics, and Mamma was a baronet's daughter, so she passed on the feminine accomplishments like drawing and music."

He frowned. "What the devil…deuce is a baronet's granddaughter doing in this backwater, playing drudge to Thomas Black? Why didn't your mother apply to her rich relations for help, if things got so bad that she had to work as a domestic?"

His bluntness sparked resentment in Margaret's eyes, and he was more convinced than ever that the governess plan wouldn't fly. "She did, but her family had disowned her when she married Papa, and they wouldn't take her back when she was widowed. Dr. Black was the only person to offer us any help."

"Was your father such an unacceptable husband?"

Bitterness twisted Margaret's lips. "For the beautiful daughter of Sir John Macclesfield, he was. Papa had been a scholarship boy at Oxford, and he was a poor curate when he and Mamma fell in love. Her parents had arranged a match with an earl. In their view, a penniless clergyman was no substitute, even if he was a good man and he adored her. Mamma and Papa were blissfully happy in our poor seaside parish, until he drowned, mounting a rescue mission in a winter storm."

When she spoke of her parents, her voice was warm with love. Whereas Joss wanted to hunt down the unknown John Macclesfield and beat him to a pulp. "How old were you when your father died?"

"Seventeen. Mamma and I lived here together for three years, but she wasn't well and eventually a fever took her. She never recovered from losing Papa."

"You've been alone at Thorncroft Hall for the last five years?"

By heaven, Uncle Thomas wasn't going to get away with this. When he returned south, Joss intended to have some stern words with his godfather about the duty he owed his cousin, however distant the relationship.

"As I said, there's Jane. And Mr. Welby. And if the weather allows, I go to church and shop in the village."

"Boundless excitement, I'm sure," Joss said grimly. "It's no life for a young lady."

She flared up, as he knew she would. "It's an honest life."

"Undoubtedly." Honest. And lonely.

When he didn't say anything more, her spurt of

temper subsided. "Perhaps I'll like governessing. Being part of a family again."

When he bent to run his hand up Emilia's sore leg, she snorted and shied away. Guilt gnawed at him. She really was in a bad way. He shouldn't have forced her through the snow last night, but by the time he'd understood his dilemma, he was too far from the last village to turn back.

"You don't think so?" Margaret asked in a challenging tone, when the silence extended.

He straightened, smacking his hands together to knock away the dust and straw. "I'll put a compress on that fetlock." He glanced at Margaret. "I won't be able to ride her for a few days. I'll have to stay."

"I know that," she said, as if it hardly mattered. If the chit knew what was in his mind, she'd be less sanguine. "Why don't you think I'll make a good governess?"

He gestured for her to stand back while he opened the gate and stepped through into the aisle. Behind him, Emilia bent her head to the bucket and drank noisily. "I think you're perfectly capable of teaching the children."

"But?"

He shrugged. "You're devilish pretty, Margaret. No woman with a brain in her head would take a girl like you into her household."

Margaret looked appalled, whether at the compliment or the implications of impropriety, he wasn't sure. "You're suggesting I'd set out to…to flirt with the master of the house?"

He was suggesting more than that. "I'm sure your intentions would be pure."

"But I'm too young?"

"Yes." He cast her a straight look. "And pardon my frankness, even if you found a place, your outspoken attitude means you'd be unlikely to keep it."

She looked troubled. "Last night, you caught me by surprise."

"And I'm exceptionally annoying."

When she didn't reply, he laughed. "Bravo. You resisted responding to that."

She set Smith down on the floor. "Proving I have some manners."

"Hmm." He headed off to fetch more oats from the bin.

She watched him curiously. "Do you always take such interest in the hired help?"

"I do when they're as comely as you are." He returned to fill Emilia's manger to the brim.

"I wish you'd stop saying that."

He carried the bucket back to the oat bin. "Whether I say it or not, it's true."

He swore he heard her grinding her teeth, but she didn't pursue the argument. "I'll go and make you something to eat."

"Thank you. I'll check the tack room for something to put on Emilia's leg."

"Mr. Welby keeps it well stocked. But if you can't find what you want, let me know."

"Thank you," he said. "I'll see you inside in a few minutes."

She dipped into a curtsy. "Yes, sir."

Before he could protest, she marched away. The saucy sway of her hips put the lie to any lip service she paid to deference.

CHAPTER FOUR

"Good morning, Margaret."

Maggie looked up from where she fried bacon and eggs for Mr. Hale's breakfast. "Good morning, sir," she said warily, wondering why he was in the kitchens, instead of safely waiting for her to serve him upstairs in the dining room.

For the last two days, she'd mostly managed to stay out of his way, in the hope that lack of contact might discourage him from seeking her out. If they encountered each other, as they inevitably did when she gave him his meals, she'd managed to act like a servant, despite his best efforts to crack her composure.

Curse him. The house, although modest by manorial standards, was big enough to ensure that they met infrequently at other times. Three floors. Six bedrooms. A couple of public rooms of manageable size.

Two people positively rattled around inside it, and it should be easy to ignore Mr. Hale. But with every second, she was more and more conscious that an alien presence invaded her territory.

She didn't want to share more of those disturbing conversations where he effortlessly slid beneath her defenses, so she found herself treating him like a friend. He couldn't be her friend—he was a guest in the house, and she was a servant. She didn't *want* him to be her friend—she was painfully aware how unbearable the loneliness would be once he left.

At first, she'd been grateful that he hadn't made any improper advances. In that, at least, he played the gentleman, even if he wasn't a gentleman in much else. But last night, she'd woken, perspiring and restless, from dreams where Mr. Hale had behaved in a most improper fashion, and she'd surrendered to his kisses with wild abandon. As she lay staring into the thick darkness, she'd finally admitted that the prospect of Mr. Hale putting his capable hands on her was far from distasteful.

Yet more reason to shun his company and raise the barriers of rank high between them.

He wore the coat and breeches he'd had on yesterday. Of course he did. He wouldn't wear his greatcoat inside. While he might cut a formidable figure in the billowing coat, she preferred that. When he was in indoor clothes, she was far too aware that his impressive size was all brawn.

The wild mop of inky curls showed traces of a comb—just. And he'd shaved. By evening, black whiskers usually shadowed that square jaw. The nascent beard always made him look a ruffian, but something secret and female in her liked to see a touch of the pirate about big, powerful Joss Hale.

Maggie tried to tell herself it was natural to notice the details of his physical appearance, seeing he was the only other person in the house. But she couldn't help feeling that her fascination with this young, virile man was inappropriate. And dangerous.

Because he was fascinating. Since his arrival, the air crackled with energy. A good morning from that rumbling bass made her very bones vibrate. Yesterday, she'd found herself surreptitiously watching from the windows, as he'd crossed to the stables from the house. Even as she warned herself how risky it was to feed her interest.

He always moved as if he knew where he was going. To a woman who had stagnated so long in this backwater, that quality was breathtakingly attractive.

Breathtakingly attractive? She was asking for disaster.

Now she needed to shoo him out of her kitchen as quickly as possible. "I'll bring your breakfast up in a moment."

"There's no need to go to that trouble." He leaned over her shoulder and sniffed appreciatively.

She stifled the urge to sniff appreciatively herself.

The scent of healthy male animal pleased her senses even more powerfully than frying bacon. "It's no trouble," she said, without looking at him.

With Mr. Hale standing so close, she was irresistibly aware that he was so much bigger than she was. Who knew the thrill a girl could get from the contrast between her slender smallness and a huge brute of a male?

He wasn't touching her. If he was, she could protest. But the breath jammed in her throat as she imagined him bridging that tantalizing gap between them.

When he'd hoisted her about that first night, she'd wanted to slap him. How odd that since then, when she recalled how effortlessly he'd hurled her across his shoulder, her heart raced with giddy excitement.

By the time he stepped back, she was lightheaded for lack of air. Glancing down at the pan, she also saw she was close to overcooking the eggs.

"Margaret," he said gently, so that low voice sounded like distant thunder, "I'm going to eat breakfast with you. You can join me upstairs, or we can stay down here. Your choice."

Oh, how glad she was that her back was turned. Otherwise he might see the devastating effect that velvety tone had on her. She closed her eyes against the lure of his soft, impossibly deep voice.

"It's not suitable," she said, making a great showing of plating the two meals.

"Perhaps not, but I feel a fool eating up there in state, while you play at humble domestic a floor below."

"I am a humble domestic," she said, struggling to keep her voice even.

"Domestic perhaps. Humble never."

When she turned around, he was setting two places at the ancient kitchen table. She watched him in surprise, the two full plates in her hands, as she was forced to accept that she'd lost the battle of the dining locations. She'd done her best, she really had, but the temptation of his company proved too powerful. And he made her sound petty for sticking to her guns.

He poured two cups of the coffee she'd planned to take up to him. "What's wrong?"

Maggie was about to lose the battle of the discreet servant, too. But it was impossible to preserve formalities, when he was quite as determined to treat her as an equal.

"You're an unusual man, Mr. Hale."

He shrugged and pulled out her chair for her as if she was a fine lady, even if one who ate in the kitchens. "I've been called worse. For example, by you."

She frowned, not because she resented his teasing, but because the silly, dizzy girl who lurked inside her liked it too much. "Dr. Black pays me to serve."

He inclined his head toward the chair. "Then you may serve by joining me for breakfast, Miss Carr."

At least this time, he didn't call her Margaret.

"Thank you," she said, giving in gracefully, because they both knew he'd won.

She couldn't really blame him for wanting someone to talk to. Even if she worried that it might all prove too heady for a woman who had spent years training herself to solitude.

Mr. Hale circled the table to sit opposite her. For someone his size, he was light on his feet. It was a sign of a man at the peak of his fitness. He'd bounced back impressively fast from that snowy trek three nights ago.

The table was large, as were the kitchens, a reminder that this house had once bustled with activity. When he'd originally employed her mother, Dr. Black had said that he'd inherited the manor from a ne'er-do-well relation who had squandered his fortune on wild parties, featuring all kinds of debauchery. A long time ago, these empty, echoing rooms had rung to the laughter of profligate young men and expensive courtesans.

Thinking about all the wicked acts that had taken place under this roof made Maggie blush. She hid her unruly thoughts by starting to eat. As always, she'd started early, feeding the hens, milking the cow, and looking after the horses. She was hungry.

Mr. Hale seemed equally enthusiastic about his breakfast. There was something satisfying about cooking a man a good meal, then watching him enjoy it.

Stop it, Maggie. You're falling into a silly fantasy where you're part of a family. When the dream crumbles to nothing, you'll be devastated.

"It's still snowing," she said, seizing on the weather as a suitably uncontroversial topic.

"Yes. And Emilia's leg is no better. I'm sorry to impose."

She hadn't been complaining about him staying, although if she had any sense, she'd want him to move on as quickly as possible. The slightest hint of a shady reputation, and a servant became unemployable. Not that while the snow lasted, anyone was likely to intrude upon their time together.

"You're lucky you made it through."

He shrugged, a characteristic response. "It's odd. In the midst of danger, you're too busy putting one foot in front of another to realize your next breath could be your last."

"I'm glad Jane left before the worst of it. If she'd delayed even a day, she'd miss the delivery."

"When is she back?"

"After Twelfth Night, if everything goes well."

"It means a rum kind of Christmas for you, though." He glanced around with a frown. "You don't decorate for the season? I notice you haven't put up any greenery."

Maggie cringed to think he saw her as pathetically sad and lonely. With a sinking feeling, she realized that she didn't want this large, unconventionally attractive man viewing her as a charity case.

She wanted him to see her as beautiful and proud and brilliant. Equal to the sophisticated ladies she had no doubt he flirted with in London.

"I make a little…" A very little. "…more effort when Jane's here."

A knowing spark lit his eyes. "A vase of holly in the hall."

She blushed. He really had guessed how paltry her Christmas celebrations were these days. "Actually we bring it down here, seeing this is where we spend most of our time on cold days."

"And I bet Jane cut it."

Her lips twitched. "I can't remember."

"If you like, I can help you collect a bit of greenery. I hate to think of moving on and leaving the house so dull."

Sitting here, sharing breakfast, Maggie hated to think of him moving on at all. It was nice having someone close to her own age to talk to, and while she knew she was playing with fire, she liked the way he looked at her.

As if, by heaven, he found her almost as interesting as she found him.

He'd emptied his plate, so she rose and started to clear the table. "Don't you have work to do?"

He lifted his coffee, keeping those deep-set eyes glued to her every movement. She still couldn't tell their exact color. Given his night-dark hair, she guessed they must be dark too.

Odd she'd thought him so gruff and grim when he arrived. Now she looked into those rugged features, and while he was definitely rough-hewn, she saw beauty of a kind. Intelligence. Humor. Spirit.

Maggie blinked. She was staring at him like a moonling. What must he think?

Except Mr. Hale stared back. For no particular reason, her cheeks heated, and the plates in her hands started to shake.

"I've made plenty of notes so far." He sounded disconcertingly normal, while their eyes seemed to conduct another conversation entirely. "We could go out this afternoon."

She should say no, invent some task, although at this time of year, there was never a huge amount to do. But the truth was she wanted to go with him and pretend that Christmas was something to look forward to, instead of dread.

If only mistletoe grew this far north. Then perhaps he'd...

One of the dirty plates tumbled from her hand and shattered on the flagstones.

In an instant, he was on his feet and fetching the broom. "Don't move. I'll clean it up. If you're pitching crockery at me, it's time you got some fresh air."

She mustered a smile, even as her heart started to gallop with anticipation. Living here with Jane, she often forgot she was young. It was impossible to forget when she was with Mr. Hale.

"Very well."

Vivid pleasure lit his expression, as he leaned on the broom handle. "Really?"

"Really."

"Well, that's capital. I'll meet you out the front at one."

With impressive efficiency, he swept up the shards. She should tell him to stop, that this was her job, but there was something very nice about having a handsome—there, she'd admitted it—young man fussing about her welfare.

When he got the dustpan and kneeled at her feet, she had to fight not to bury her hands in that thick mop of hair. Was it crisp or soft? Warm or cool?

She bit her lip against the surge of curiosity and made herself speak. Silences were becoming a little too meaningful. "You seem to know what you're doing."

His wry smile had her heart doing somersaults. "Did you think I was a useless ornament to society?"

No, she didn't. She'd seen the way he cared for Emilia and fed her animals. She suspected he was impressively competent in everything he did. Including how he touched a woman's body.

Maggie was blushing again. She hoped to heaven he wouldn't notice.

This improper situation filled her head with all

kinds of improper thoughts. Thoughts she'd never had before.

And the most improper thought of all was that she started to hope it kept snowing into the next century.

Mr. Hale went on, which was a relief. She was having trouble finding her voice. "I work for my living, I'll have you know. And I've had to fend for myself for years."

"In that case, you don't need me to run after you."

He raised his eyes, and at last she saw what color they were. A dark, serpentine green like the sea under a rocky overhang. The erratic breath jammed in her lungs, and she had a strange feeling that she plunged headfirst into that deep green sea. Down. Down. Until she feared she might never come up again.

She waited for him to smile, but he looked deadly serious. "No, I want you here. You, my girl, are not going anywhere."

Oh, my...

Because heaven forgive her, while her buzzing ears heard every word, her reeling senses heard only three.

I want you.

CHAPTER FIVE

Joss waited for Margaret in the snowy yard. He felt on edge, the way he had the very first time he'd asked a girl to take a walk with him. Which was absurd, when then he'd been a stripling of thirteen, and now he was a grown man approaching thirty.

But the same suspense tightened his gut. The same anticipation sharpened his senses.

If he was honest, this was worse. The word at Eton had been that the bandmaster's daughter was generous with her favors and would kiss any fellow behind the cricket pavilion in exchange for sixpence.

Miss Margaret Carr was made of sterner stuff.

Except this morning for a few tremulous seconds, she hadn't looked stern at all. Instead she'd looked like a young girl stepping out of the shadows to discover a new world. And even better, she trusted Joss Hale to show her.

Since leaving her downstairs, he'd wandered the house in a daze. He hadn't noted a single fine cornice or ill-favored window. Instead he'd seen the soft light entering those perfect blue eyes as she'd watched him kneeling at her feet.

For a few mad moments, he'd wanted to say that he kneeled in worship, not because, much more prosaically, he cleared up a broken plate.

"Will she come, Bob?" he asked the stocky pony he'd harnessed to the cart he'd found in the stables. "Or will she think better of it?"

Bob, an affectionate creature, he'd discovered, butted him with his head and whickered.

"No, I'm not sure either."

If Margaret deigned to spend the afternoon with Joss, he needed to remember her innocence. Because he couldn't pretend that he was still that unworldly schoolboy. He knew what that soft flush on a lovely face meant. He even knew why she'd dropped the plate.

She wasn't immune to the attraction flaring between them. If she were, she wouldn't be nearly so jumpy. But while he might know the steps, this particular dance could only lead her to disaster.

He checked his pocket watch. It wasn't one o'clock yet. Impatience ate at him. He'd been early for the bandmaster's daughter, too.

At least the snow had stopped. Although if the weather cleared, honor dictated that he leave Thorncroft Hall and delay his return until this one too beguiling girl had more company.

Joss heard her boots squeak in the snow, and his heart rose as he turned to see her tramping toward him. He couldn't remember the last time he'd found a female so bedazzling.

When had he started to lose his enthusiasm for the chase?

Perhaps he was spoiled. He was far from handsome, and his manners were atrocious. Not to mention he was the size of a barn. But he'd never had any trouble attracting women. Whereas Margaret was making him work for her favors.

"My goodness." She stared at the cart. "You're taking this seriously."

He gestured toward the basket hanging off her arm. "You're not."

She smiled, and his heart performed one of those flips that were becoming almost commonplace in her presence.

Margaret was completely bundled up against the cold. Thick coat, gloves, shawl wrapped around her head, giving the barest hint of the rich red hair that colored his dreams. The only part of her left uncovered was her piquant face.

Yet Joss found himself more powerfully seduced

than he'd ever been by a reckless widow, welcoming him into her bed and wearing the merest whisper of silk.

Despite the cold, his blood warmed at the thought of Margaret wearing a whisper of silk.

"Remember that anything that goes up has to come down after Twelfth Night, and the person most likely to be cleaning up is me."

He wanted to say that he'd be here, too. That he'd never leave.

Which was utterly mad. The house, however lovely, was in the middle of nowhere. He'd known the girl for three days.

A fortnight ago, he'd come close to quarreling with his mother, when he'd said he wasn't coming home for Christmas because he couldn't tolerate her matchmaking. Yet right now, if some angel floated down and asked him what he wanted for Christmas, he'd say he wanted to look at Margaret Carr until the day he died.

Sheer lunacy.

Joss summoned a light tone—more difficult than he'd expected—and sent the girl a mocking glance. "Tch. Tch. It's poor spirited to be so hardheaded at Christmastime. If all we did was worry about cleaning up, we'd never do a damned thing."

She frowned, although laughter still danced in those lovely eyes. "Your family will miss you. You're clearly the king of Christmas."

He should feel guilty. They would miss him, especially his mother, who loved nothing better than getting the whole family under one roof for the Festive Season. It would seem odd, not going down to the old house on the Sussex Downs, the house that had first sparked his love for fine architecture.

"I'd rather be here with you," he said, before he could stop himself.

Maggie looked startled. "Thank you." She considered his statement further. "I think."

He spoke quickly to gloss over the sudden awkwardness. "If anywhere needs a visit from the king of Christmas, it's Thorncroft. Why, when I arrived, you wouldn't know it was the Festive Season at all. Not a ribbon. Not a garland. Not even so much as an echo of a carol. It's like the house Christmas forgot."

"Well, you're fixing that," she said drily.

He reached over to take her basket and toss it into the back of the cart. "See? I note a hint of cynicism. That's the sort of attitude we have to change. And fast. Clearly this is a Christmas emergency, and that's why fate has sent me to your door. There's no time to be lost. Point me to the woodlands."

Maggie laughed. And found herself laughing again and again, as she and Mr. Hale wandered the snowy woods behind the house in search of greenery. She'd thought they'd cut a few sprigs of holly before they headed home, but the cart was soon laden with boughs of pine and holly, enough to make the whole house bright.

The weather held while they were outside. Now and again, there was a glimmer of pale sunlight through the thick clouds. But as they turned back to the manor, the snow started again.

She turned her face up to the flakes and out of childish habit, stuck her tongue out to catch a couple. When she realized Mr. Hale was watching her, she blushed at her nonsense.

"It's supposed to be lucky," she said defensively.

"I hadn't heard that." He stared at her as if he'd never seen a woman before.

"Mamma and I used to play games in the snow. I don't know if it's a real superstition or not, but we always did it." Her eyes flickered down, then up again. "You must think I'm silly."

He smiled at her, and her foolish heart stuttered, although surely only the fading light lent such tenderness to his expression. "It's nice to see you being a bit silly. You mostly seem to take life very earnestly."

She should tell him to mind his own business. But she found herself responding honestly. "In recent years, I haven't had much fun. We used to. Papa was a very jolly vicar. Everyone loved him, and his parishioners were devastated when he died. They wanted us to stay in the village, but they were so poor themselves, we couldn't take their charity. Mamma and I continued to celebrate Christmas after we came here. I just…I just seem to have got out of the habit." She smiled at Joss. "Thank you for reminding me that it's the season of goodwill, not the season for sitting around feeling sorry for yourself."

"You're such a sparkling girl." Her gratitude didn't seem to please him. Instead he looked troubled. "You should have the world at your feet."

She fought to keep her smile in place, although she cringed at the poor figure she cut with her lack of sophistication and drab clothes. When she'd give anything to dazzle him with her wit and beauty.

And all was not lost. He'd called her sparkling.

"Well, I do have the king of Christmas in my thrall," she said lightly.

To her surprise, he touched her cheek with one leather-gloved hand. The contact was over in an instant. Surely she must imagine the blast of heat sizzling through her, heat that made a mockery of the freezing air.

"You do at that," he said softly.

Her lungs stopped working, and she found herself enmeshed in his gaze, unable to break free.

Bob shattered the stasis. He butted his square head against Mr. Hale's arm, protesting at standing still while the temperature plummeted. Maggie watched Mr. Hale come back to reality, as he turned to rub the pony's nose.

Bob was clearly his devoted slave. Joss Hale had a gift for inspiring affection, Maggie had noticed. She hated to think she was quite as susceptible as the pony was to the man's disheveled charms, but she suspected she was. Right now after her happiest hours in years, she couldn't summon the will to resist a fall that began to seem inevitable.

"We're too slow for Bob." Maggie caught a faint huskiness in Mr. Hale's voice that hinted he, too, had felt that strange connection with her.

He started to walk back toward the house, one hand holding Bob's bridle, not that he needed leading. The pony had been born on this estate. Maggie fell into step beside them. An unexpectedly tranquil silence descended, broken only by the crunch of feet in the snow. The rest of the world lay hushed beneath the curtain of white.

When she stumbled over a branch buried in the snow, Mr. Hale took her arm, and she didn't pull away.

"There's another Christmas superstition in the valley," she said, after they'd covered most of the way back.

"Oh?"

"Yes. If a stranger crosses your threshold in Advent, it means good luck."

He gave a soft huff of laughter. "I hope to God that's true."

"I'm sure it is."

But was she? When he left, she'd feel lonelier than

ever. She'd barely endured her humdrum life, when she'd had nothing to compare it to. But after a mere three days in the company of this vigorous, attractive man, she already knew that Thorncroft would feel like a desert when Mr. Hale was gone.

CHAPTER SIX

"$\mathcal{L}$ook what I found," Mr. Hale said, coming back into the hall from the kitchens, where he'd gone to fetch a basket for the pine cones they'd collected yesterday.

Maggie turned from tweaking the holly she was arranging above the huge stone fireplace. They'd spent the morning decorating the hall. The formerly bare and unwelcoming space was now green and fragrant, and redolent of the season. All the other downstairs rooms sported vases crammed with holly.

"We should get a Yule log," she said.

He laughed. "For someone who needed to be coaxed into celebrating Christmas, you're getting into the spirit of things. We'll fix it up tonight, when we come back from skating."

"From what?" Then she noticed what dangled from

those large, adept hands. "Oh, you found the skates. I'd forgotten we had them."

"I didn't know Uncle Thomas indulged."

"I think the previous owner must have left them behind." Although skating seemed an innocuous occupation for that wild young buck, given what she'd heard about him.

"Well, shall we?"

She shot the skates a doubtful look. "I haven't been on the ice since I was a child."

He took both sets of skates in one hand and extended his other hand toward her. "I won't let you fall."

She wished she could be so certain. And she wasn't talking about sliding around on the ice.

Since yesterday, she'd given up any pretense of keeping Mr. Hale at a distance. This morning, he'd touched her often, seemingly casual little contacts, helping her carry things, or lifting her down off the ladder. And she, knowing the risks she took, hadn't said a word to deter him.

Perhaps she was already skating after all—on very thin ice indeed.

Maggie might be inexperienced, but she wasn't stupid. She knew a girl asked for trouble when she encouraged a young man to touch her and smile at her and spend time alone with her.

"It might be fun." She stepped forward and took his

hand, loving the way those long fingers wrapped around hers.

He was so warm. That was irresistible on a cold day like this. Goodness, it was irresistible in a cold life like hers.

She was falling, whatever promises he made to her. And she wasn't doing much to save herself.

"Is there a pond?" The spark of approval in his green eyes made her heart swell with happiness. "There must be, or they wouldn't have skates here."

"There's one that freezes solid most winters. Shall we go and see?"

"Get changed, and I'll meet you down here."

She rushed upstairs on feet that flew, because she didn't want to be away from Mr. Hale any longer than she needed to be. After all, she'd be without him for a long time once he left her.

There was something evocative about silent woods where the only tracks belonged to wild creatures like deer and pheasants and rabbits. It was still freezing, but the snow overnight hadn't been as heavy.

The pond, as Joss expected in this magic kingdom, was perfect for skating. Long, and wide enough for acrobatics should he decide to show off, and fringed with willows turned to white lace with frost. A thick branch even extended over the ice, ideal for them to sit on while they strapped on their skates.

Slipping a little, he ventured out to test the thickness, but a lifetime's skating with his family already told him that the ice would easily bear the weight of two people.

Margaret hovered on the bank, looking uncharacteristically nervous. Carefully he made his way back to her. The ice was deuced slippery, which boded well for a good afternoon's sport.

She was bundled up again, like she'd been yesterday. When he reached out to take one gloved hand, he was pleased at how readily she accepted his touch.

He'd been touching her most of the day. The pleasure had soon turned to torture. Because the brief, chaste contacts weren't enough. He wanted more than to place a hand at her waist to steady her as she climbed up to drape ivy over a picture, or suffer the cool brush of her fingers as she passed him the scissors.

His fingers itched to linger and explore. His arms ached to draw her close. He burned to kiss her.

Hell, he wanted to do much more than that.

Margaret had no idea how close he'd come this morning to slamming her up against the wall and kissing her to the edge of madness.

But every time his desire threatened to overmaster his honor, she looked at him with such shy trust that he couldn't do it. She was looking at him like that now.

"Don't tell me you're scared," Joss said in gentle reproof.

She cast an uncertain glance at the pond. "I'd much rather watch you."

"Not good enough. I'll hold your hand."

More torture, not that he had any intention of denying himself the privilege. He squeezed her fingers in silent encouragement and pulled her toward the branch over the pond. When she resisted, he looked back with a smile.

"Don't be a goose, Margaret. A woman who can defend her castle from a great brute of an invader can't be scared of a little ice."

"But I didn't. The brute got in anyway."

Yes, he had, hadn't he? "You're wittering again, my girl."

Spreading his feet to keep his balance, he caught her round the waist and lifted her across to sit on the branch.

She scowled at him with adorable displeasure. "You can't win every argument by grabbing me and putting me where you want me."

"Why not? So far, it's working." He returned to collect the skates from the bank. "And don't think of moving."

"You're such a bully," she said without heat.

He smiled. "You just don't like anyone else giving orders. Are you going to let me put on your skates?"

"If you insist."

"Good." Taking off his gloves, he dipped to his knees. When he lifted her foot, it looked absurdly dainty in his hold, despite the sensible half-boot. He took a moment to admire her shapely ankle in its black woolen stocking. Deftly he buckled on the skate. Then he repeated the action for the other foot.

"Stay there," he said, his voice gruff as he fought the urge to bury his face in her lap. It was cold enough to freeze the balls off a polar bear, yet Joss felt so hot, he could explode.

He sat beside Margaret, and this time was cautious enough to keep his distance. All this agony was to no purpose, even if she said yes—and that was as likely as that freezing polar bear dancing a gavotte. He could hardly seduce the girl on a snowy bank.

Once his skates were on and he'd replaced his gloves, he stood and launched into a powerful glide across the ice. He came to a stop and twirled several times before facing her. It seemed he did want to show off.

Her face was alight with admiration. "My goodness, you look at home."

He skated in and held out his hands. "Come on. You'll like it."

Inevitably his mind focused on something else she'd like. To his relief, she wobbled so badly on her skates, he had to put his licentious thoughts aside and concentrate on saving her from toppling over.

"Go slowly," she said, at last finding a tottering balance.

"I won't do anything you don't want me to."

Devil take it, did everything he said have to sound like an invitation to bed sport?

He stared into her eyes and waited for her to stand up straight and steady. Very slowly, he backed out onto the pond.

As he'd expected, she soon found her feet, and the deathly clutch on his hands loosened. "Better?"

She nodded, although the tense line of her lush mouth told him she wasn't yet at ease. "Yes."

"Can I let go of one hand?"

Shakily she released his hand, and for a few moments, they skated side by side. With every minute, she gained in confidence. Gradually he built the pace, until they glided smooth and graceful across the ice and the wind lifted his hair.

He glanced at her face and was delighted to see pleasure had replaced terror. Her cheeks were flushed, and her remarkable eyes were bright. He drew her around in a great swooping arc that sent her skirts belling out.

"You've remembered how," he said, as she stopped beside him with breathtaking skill.

"I'd forgotten what fun it is."

"We've hardly started," he said, wanting to show her every pleasure in the world. And for once, he wasn't thinking about what he wanted to do to her in his bed.

Right now, in her dowdy winter clothes, she was the loveliest woman he'd ever seen. He'd met society's beauties, and none could hold a candle to Margaret Carr on this hidden, icy pond in the depths of wildest Yorkshire.

He caught her free hand and turned around fast, surprising an excited laugh from her. Then he caught her waist and skated swift as an arrow down the pond. And damn him, if she didn't keep up. When they reached the end, she pulled away to skate free. For breathless minutes, he pursued her as she swung off, laughing. When he reached her, he spun her into a wild waltz.

He'd always remember these blissful hours, dancing across the pond with Margaret. Meeting. Parting. Meeting again. Touching. Breaking away.

The short winter day drew in around them, but he couldn't bring himself to leave the ice.

Until finally he caught her by the waist and deliberately overbalanced into a thick snowbank rising above the edge of the pond.

Laughing, she tumbled down beside him, gripping his hand tight. "Oh, that was a rotten thing to do."

Breathlessly he struggled up on one elbow so he could lean over her and stare into her unforgettable face. He watched the laughter fade from her eyes, as they darkened with sensual awareness.

Knowing he broke every rule, but unable to resist, Joss lowered his head and placed his lips on hers.

CHAPTER SEVEN

aggie knew Joss was going to kiss her. She even had time to say the words that would tell him not to.

Except she'd wanted him to kiss her since the moment skating had turned into flying.

No, that was a lie. She'd wanted him to kiss her yesterday, when they'd had such fun in the woods, cutting the greenery for the house.

Fun…

Who knew what fun *fun* could be?

Today had been fun, too. But fun spiced with a physical awareness that made every word, every touch feel like the gateway to some profound transformation. When his lips, a delicious mixture of cold and heat, met hers, she arched up in silent welcome. She slid her arm around his neck, knocking his hat off into the snow.

He gave a muffled grunt of amusement against her

lips, before everything changed to dark delight. The warmth of his lips turned her bones to liquid, as she sank into a new and glorious world.

She'd never been kissed before. Her first reaction was surprise at the intimacy. Sharing breath with Joss felt like sharing her soul. Then more surprise when he nipped at her lower lip. The brief sting sent a shock of pleasure rushing through her.

She gasped. And gasped again when the tip of his tongue slipped through to taste her. He made a sound of appreciation deep in his throat and lifted her higher against his body. This was like being in a bear's embrace. He was so big and hot and strong, and she felt so deliciously fragile in his arms.

Fragile, yet strangely powerful.

She flexed gloved hands against the curls at his nape, striving to etch each sensation into her memory. In the lonely years to come, she would take out this exquisite moment and relive every detail. The subtle movement of his lips, soft yet demanding. The scent of his skin, warm male and sharp air. The press of the snow at her back. The way his arms lashed her into his chest as if he never wanted to let her go.

This time when his tongue flicked along the seam of her lips, Maggie opened to him. Immediately the kiss changed, flaring from gentle exploration to urgent demand.

When he slid his tongue into her mouth, she gave a muffled whimper. But the strangeness faded as desire burgeoned. A deep, insistent throbbing started between her legs, and she instinctively tilted her hips toward him.

Joss groaned and sucked her tongue into his mouth. Despite her innocence, Maggie recognized a blatant invitation to imitate how he kissed her. Feeling daring, she flicked her tongue along his. His salty taste flooded her senses and made her blood pump with wanton heat. She buried her hands in his hair and gave herself up to him.

His hands stroked along her body, until the barrier of clothing between them became unbearable. She made a soft sound of discontent and bowed up to press against him. His hand caught her breast, and despite all those layers of wool, the shock of the contact made her stiffen. Her nipple tightened in swift, aching demand for more.

"Hell," he muttered and wrenched away to collapse flat on his back beside her.

Maggie didn't immediately move, although the snow had started to seep through her thick clothing. His kisses had been so intoxicating, she lay lost in a dream of delight. Her lips tingled from the cold air and the pressure of his.

Then she turned her head and was dismayed to see how wretched he looked. "Joss?"

"We shouldn't have done that." She'd never heard him sound so grim.

Oh, dear Lord. Had she done something to

displease him? She'd loved his kisses, but perhaps her inexperienced enthusiasm had disgusted him.

Feeling sick, she pushed herself up on her elbows, the better to read his expression. Then was sorry that she had. He looked tormented, and deep lines bracketed his mouth.

"I thought…I thought you liked it," she said in a shaky voice.

He stared up at the trees, as if they held the answer to all his questions. "Of course I bloody liked it," he bit out. "Too much."

She frowned, not understanding how his ardor had changed so quickly to this bitterness. "Then why are you angry with me?"

His lips turned down in self-derision. "I'm not angry with you."

She shivered at his curt tone. As the afternoon drew in, the air grew colder. When Joss had kissed her, she'd foolishly imagined she'd never feel cold again. "Then what's wrong?"

At last he looked at her. The green eyes were dull and unhappy. "You're not that innocent, Margaret."

"Please call me Maggie," she said quickly, even as she acknowledged that he was right to accuse her of being disingenuous about what they'd done. That hadn't been a quick, flirtatious kiss to mark the end of a couple of enjoyable hours together. Those kisses said that he meant to bed her.

"Maggie." The edge he lent the word in no way

conveyed fondness, yet hearing him speak her name for the first time flooded her with forbidden pleasure. "From the moment I met you, I wanted to kiss you."

Shocked, she sat up fully and studied his features. So far she'd known him as a lighthearted companion. But this man regarding her with somber green eyes was a more powerful adversary than she'd ever imagined.

Adversary? Why on earth did she call him that?

He wasn't her enemy. Even if right now, his stare held no hint of softness.

She shivered again. Nothing to do with the worsening cold. Heaven help her, this new version of Joss Hale was even more compelling than the cheerful, charming companion she'd come to know over the last few days.

And she'd already lost her heart to that man.

Her breath cramped in her lungs. Oh, surely that wasn't true. It couldn't be true. Could someone fall in love in four days?

She drank in the sight of him, imprinting him deep in her heart, and recognized that she could. She had.

"Have I frightened you?" he asked in that austere tone. He raised one knee and rested his arm on it, still watching her like a cat watched a mouse hole.

She shook her head. "No."

At her swift denial, the flat line of his lips relaxed a fraction. "I'm glad." He sucked in an audible breath.

"But now I have kissed you, I need to leave. You see that, don't you?"

She bit back a cry to think of him going away. "Do you mean I'll never see you again?"

"I'll come back to you, Maggie. Once Jane gets home."

"But it won't be the same." She bit her lip and stared out across the ice, blinking hard, telling herself she wouldn't cry. "I'll be the housekeeper, and you'll be the guest. We won't be…alone."

She glanced back in time to catch a hunted expression crossing his face. "It's us being alone that's the problem."

"Nobody knows," she said quickly. "Nobody needs to know."

"And what if I can't keep my hands off you?" he asked roughly. "Are you ready to share my bed, Maggie? Because if I stay, that's exactly where you're going to end up."

She returned stare for stare. "You don't imagine I can resist you?"

He shook his head, and at last a hint of his characteristic wry humor appeared. "We can't resist each other, my darling." They no longer touched, but she'd never been so conscious of another person's nearness. "Or are you going to pretend that's not true?"

Denying his statement would be too coy for words. This attraction had existed from the start, strengthening with every moment they'd spent together since.

"No. It's true," she said in a subdued voice.

Triumph flashed in his eyes, and he reached toward her. She leaned in, only to watch him draw away before he made contact.

"If I touch you, I won't stop," he said, and she flinched at the bleakness in his tone.

What was the point of arguing? He knew how vulnerable she was to him. "I won't want you to stop," she muttered miserably, raising her knees and clasping her shaking hands around them.

"You see?" With unusually clumsy movements, he began to unfasten his skates. "I'll go back to the house and pack my things."

"You can't go tonight." She grabbed his arm, as if meaning to keep him by force.

Gently he caught her hand and untangled it from his black sleeve. "I have to."

"But it will be dark in a few hours, and I can smell snow in the air."

How she hated the whine in her voice. Even more she hated the thought of wandering around an empty house that Joss's company had briefly turned into a home.

A muscle worked in that lean cheek. "You said it's five miles to the village."

"There's nowhere to stay," Maggie said in a thick voice, as she fumbled to unfasten her skates. "I told you. The nearest inn is in Tolbeath, and you won't get there tonight."

He picked up his hat from the snow and placed it on his disheveled dark head. "Someone in Little Flitwick will take me in."

"And ask questions. Wouldn't it be better to stay tonight?"

Wouldn't it be better to stay forever?

But she quailed from asking that question. Joss was attracted to her, she knew, but that didn't mean he wanted more than a quick tumble. They'd only met four days ago, after all.

So what exactly did she want of him, apart from more kisses? Passion that went beyond kisses? Stirring, forbidden pictures of Joss's big body moving above hers in the act of love invaded her mind. A yearning so sharp, it verged on excruciating made her blood spike.

But for all her brave words, she wasn't ready to forsake the code of a lifetime and share his bed until he returned to London.

She couldn't be his mistress. Did that mean she awaited a proposal?

That stretched the limits of the possible. Outside the world of fairytales, handsome princes didn't wed humble maidservants and sweep them back to their palaces for a life of happily ever after.

Even if Joss contemplated a commitment, she was agonizingly aware of the gulf stretching between them. They might come from similar backgrounds, but over the years, she'd sunk a long way down in the world. It was perfectly clear that Josiah Hale could look higher for a bride than a penniless servant.

And how did Maggie know that he cared for her beyond a fleeting interest? While all of this was deathly serious to her, he might make a habit of flirting with chance-met girls on his travels. Perhaps she was another forgettable encounter among many.

But staring deep into his green eyes, she knew that was unfair. For the sake of her reputation, he was about to undertake a difficult, dangerous journey. He understood how much hung upon his actions.

Joss Hale was a man of honor. He recoiled at the prospect of ruining a virtuous woman.

The problem for the virtuous woman was his resolve only made him more appealing.

Holding the skates by their straps, he rose to loom over her. "Maggie, I don't trust myself if I stay." He sounded as miserable as she did. Whatever this attraction was between them, it was significant. For him as well as her. "You're a vicar's daughter. Giving yourself to me goes against everything you've been taught."

When he extended his hand toward her, she didn't immediately take it. Although if she sat here much longer, the snow would soak through to her petticoats. She avoided his eyes and rubbed her gloved hands together to hide their trembling.

"I know," she said in a low voice.

Every week in church, she spoke the words, entreating the Lord not to lead her into temptation.

She'd never before understood what temptation meant. Dear heaven above, she started to understand now.

Temptation, large, intriguing, irresistible, stood there, watching her, as if he read every wicked longing in her heart. "Come back to the house."

She blinked back more tears and struggled to tell herself that she made too much of this. What she felt for Joss must be a passing madness. He was the first man to kiss her, the first man to treat her like an attractive woman. No wonder she imagined herself in love with him.

A mere four days couldn't change her forever. And the Margaret Carr who was her parents' daughter would never crawl into a stranger's bed, just because she'd discovered the power of a man's caresses. She was made of stronger stuff than that.

Maggie lifted her chin and turned to face Joss with a smile on her face. "Thank you for a lovely afternoon —I'd forgotten how much fun skating is."

He didn't smile back. She suspected she hadn't managed much of a smile at that, but she was doing her best. Instead something that looked mortifyingly like compassion softened his green gaze to jade. "It's been a wonderful few days, Maggie. I'll never be sorry I found you."

Unfortunately, she could imagine being very sorry indeed. She was a prisoner granted temporary freedom, but who faced a return to grim captivity. Her chains would weigh twice as heavy, now she'd tasted the sweetness of liberty.

Oh, dear. It was bad enough Joss feeling sorry for her. She didn't need to add her own self-pity to the mix. It was time to count her blessings, and stop crying for the moon.

She was safe and sheltered. She'd shared kisses to build her dreams upon. And now she knew how it felt to have a man shaking with desire for her. A man she wanted.

The problem was that while Joss was here, she didn't want to waste time storing up memories. She was too greedy for every moment of his company to worry about looking ahead to when he was gone. She wanted more of the raw, passionate experience.

If wishes were horses, beggars would ride.

The bleak little aphorism didn't lift her spirits. With a heart that felt weighted down with bricks, she accepted his hand and let him pull her to her feet. After gliding over the ice like a bird in flight, trudging home through the snow seemed an uninspiring way to travel.

Enough of the countrywoman remained for her to wish him on his way before darkness fell. He'd have a bad enough time reaching Little Flitwick in the remaining daylight.

He must go, although Maggie loathed admitting it. Big, echoing Thorncroft Hall was too small to keep her apart from Joss, if they remained alone together under its roof.

CHAPTER EIGHT

Joss strapped the last of his bags to Emilia's saddle and gave her a pat to apologize. "I'm sorry, old girl. I know you're not eager to be on your way. I'm not either."

She whickered in response and bless her generous heart, followed readily enough when he led her out of her stall and into the aisle through the center of the stables.

Ahead, he could see the lowering late afternoon sky through the open doors. Maggie was right about the weather. The smell of snow lay sharp on the air.

Then a sight more dangerous by far than any bad weather appeared in the doorway.

"How is Emilia's leg?" Maggie asked, coming into the stables but keeping her distance. Like him, she'd changed into dry clothes.

Joss hadn't seen the woman who haunted his every

thought since they'd returned to the house after skating. He'd gone upstairs to pack his few things, and she'd disappeared into the kitchens, he assumed. Downstairs anyway.

He'd guessed she avoided farewells. If she felt the way he did, like someone scraped out his liver with a rusty pitchfork, he couldn't blame her.

By God, he didn't want to go. That reluctance was yet another sign that he must. And quickly.

His mother would be damned proud of him. If he ever told her about the lost, enchanted days in this hidden valley. Which of course he never would.

"She'll carry me as far as the village," he said, although he feared he might be too optimistic. Emilia had stopped limping yesterday, but she was a long way from full fitness.

"You could take Bob."

"Then questions would be asked."

"Oh, that's right." A wry smile curled Maggie's lips and made him want to kiss her. Hell, he always wanted to kiss her. Now he'd actually done it, he was hungrier than ever. "I'm not very good at romantic intrigue."

"The weather's closing in." And the night. What he'd give to be looking forward to lying in a nice warm bed beside Maggie, instead of tramping through a snowstorm. "I must go."

"Yes, you must." She didn't move.

Nor did he. "I wondered whether you'd decided not to say goodbye."

"I wouldn't be such a coward." Her shaking hand held out a small bundle. "I prepared some food. And I put a flask of Dr. Black's best brandy in there, too."

"Thank you." Joss took the bundle and turned to pack it into his saddlebag with his sketchbooks. He had a few ideas for modernizing the house. But mostly he wanted to leave it as it was. It was lovely and unique and unspoiled. Like the woman who lived in it.

"I will come back, I swear," he said into Emilia's flank.

"I hope so," Maggie said, and at last he heard her voice wobble.

It shouldn't gratify him to know she grieved over his departure, but of course it did. When he rode away, he wanted her bawling her eyes out. He wanted her to cry until the triumphant day he galloped back down the drive and took her into his arms. That was how much of a bastard he was.

Joss turned to face her and immediately felt like a swine for wishing her unhappy. The misery in her expression twisted his gut.

You're leaving for her sake.

But the words rapidly lost any power. So rapidly that if he didn't leave right now, he wouldn't.

"There's something I need to do first," he said with sudden decision.

She frowned at him in puzzlement. "What?"

"This."

He grabbed her by the waist and hauled her up against him.

Maggie gave a shocked squeak, followed by a delicious sigh of surrender as his mouth crashed down onto hers. When he'd kissed her in the snow, she'd been shy and uncertain, although she'd worked out the basics with impressive speed.

This time, he made no allowance for her inexperience and plundered her mouth with all the passion she stirred in his soul. She moaned into his mouth and twined around him, holding him like she never wanted to go another day without having him near.

Joss held onto her too long. He held onto her not nearly long enough.

He wrenched away, curling his hands around her arms to keep her upright as she sagged toward him. He didn't feel too secure on his feet himself.

"Remember that, Maggie," he said almost savagely. "Remember that, until I come back to you."

She stared at him with wide blue eyes and didn't speak as he flung himself on Emilia's back and urged the mare into the cold air.

Joss didn't look back. He didn't trust himself to keep going if he did.

For a long time, Maggie stood in the stable doorway and looked out over the snowy hills surrounding the estate. Because of the lie of the land, she couldn't see Joss as he rode down the drive and turned onto the road across the fields, the road that would eventually take him to the outside world. That outside world would quickly claim him back as its own, so he'd forget whatever charms he imagined he'd found in Fraedale.

As she waited, the afternoon grew colder, and it started to snow. Stamping her booted feet to restore circulation, she wrapped her shawl more closely about her, but didn't think of going inside to the warmth.

Not yet.

The wind whistled around her ears and stung her cheeks and eyes. She wasn't crying, but with every second that passed, the sorrow that lodged in her stomach expanded. Until it was the size of a boulder. Until it was the size of a mountain, ready to tumble down and crush her to nothing.

She bit her lip, without looking away from the empty hills. Already she missed Joss so much. At last, she understood the true cruelty of her situation.

She'd been lonely for years. Since she'd left her father's vicarage after his death. Worse since her mother passed away.

But Joss's absence was a physical pain, a crippling loss. Loneliness bit far more viciously, when it focused on one desired person.

Finally she saw what she wanted—dreaded—to see. The light was nearly gone, but against the snowy landscape of the high hills, the man leading his horse was clearly visible.

Joss must have decided to walk to save Emilia's leg. Maggie frowned. If he ran into bad weather with a lame horse, he mightn't reach the village.

"Dear God, keep him safe," she whispered into the dusty, hay-scented shadows gathering around her. Her breath formed clouds in the freezing air. "Keep him safe, even if he forgets me and never comes back."

The sound of a human voice after the long silence made Bob whicker from his stall. Smith twined around Maggie's legs, with a plaintive miaow to say she hadn't been fed since Easter.

Still Maggie watched as the man and his horse climbed up toward the pass and disappeared over the brow of the hill.

He'd gone. And with his leaving, all the warmth and laughter and joy—and, yes, the promise of passion—had gone, too. If Maggie's life had felt bleak before Joss's arrival, now it seemed unbearably barren.

She struggled to find the will to move, to put one foot in front of another. Smith complained again, and she bent to stroke the cat's black and white head.

Duty called. Emotional devastation didn't change that.

Feeling as though she was ninety years old and every movement hurt, she settled the animals for the night. As she crossed the yard toward the house, it started to snow. How she hoped Joss was approaching shelter.

Back in the kitchen, she slumped onto the settle in front of the roaring fire. It was nearly dinnertime, but she didn't do anything about preparing a meal. The thought of food made her stomach curdle. Smith curled up on her lap and bore Maggie's sobs with good grace—for a cat.

She could live without Joss. She'd only known him four days. That shouldn't be long enough to change her whole future. A few kisses, some companionship, a compatible soul to share laughter. None of these things were necessary for survival. Although they'd been so very nice.

She'd go on. She had to.

And perhaps in time, he would come back as he promised.

But the precious intimacy they'd found during these snowy days would never return. The bond between them had been a product of their isolation.

Most likely Joss wouldn't come back, and she'd continue as she had before. It would be as if nothing had happened. Because in the world's eyes, nothing had. Nobody would ever know she and Joss had shared this house without the benefit of a chaperone. There would be no local gossip about the naughty house-keeper up at Thorncroft Hall, and what she'd got up to with the London visitor. Even if Joss had left her as innocent as when he'd arrived.

Or almost.

She remained a virtuous woman. Her chastity had been assailed, and she'd emerged triumphant.

Maggie didn't feel triumphant. She felt bereft and alone. Anger beat back her despair as she fumbled for her handkerchief and blew her nose.

Twenty-five years of spotless propriety, and what did she have to show for it? Her good reputation and respectably preserved virginity didn't make her any happier.

She'd never imagined resenting the moral strictures she'd always obeyed. But as she sat forlorn in an empty house, when she could be enjoying Joss's kisses and lying in Joss's bed, her choice didn't seem nearly so clear-cut.

Joss had guessed how close she verged to throwing over her principles. He hadn't left just because he feared for his own restraint. He'd left because he knew that Maggie hovered a kiss away from surrender.

She'd never learned how to dissemble, and he was a perceptive man. He must guess she was falling in love with him. To his credit, he'd done the only thing a man of honor could do. He'd gone.

And to her credit, she'd let him go.

She didn't feel much like patting herself on the back. Instead she felt like her courage had failed her when she'd most needed it. As a result, she'd made the greatest mistake of her life.

Oh, she knew the price of following the primrose

path. The fishing village in Kent had its share of fallen women and bastard children. And her gentle, loving parents would never understand why she might go against everything they'd taught her to believe.

But love had its own imperatives. And sitting in front of the fire on her own—and facing a life that promised more solitude—she couldn't help thinking that sin might have its compensations.

The lantern revealed an endless fall of white against the blackness. Joss sensed the hillsides crowding closer and closer as he approached the pass. The wind howled about him with an inhuman shriek. Despite the protection of his hat, icy water trickled down the back of his neck. Beneath his booted feet, the road was treacherous with ice. Behind him, Emilia continued to make awkward progress, favoring her lame leg.

"Not far now, girl," he said, but the gale whipped his words away.

Probably a good thing. They were a damned lie.

He'd thought he was cold the night he stumbled onto Thorncroft Hall, more a matter of good luck than good judgment. It didn't compare to this icy hell. Yet he couldn't be much more than a mile away from the hall.

He staggered into a thick snowdrift and only kept his balance by wrenching at Emilia's rein. He rapidly reached a stage where rational thought failed. One stubborn vow played over and over in his head.

I must leave Maggie. It's for her own good.

I must leave Maggie. It's for her own good.

Each grim syllable tolled like a dirge, as he lumbered onto the road that took him back to his real life.

His real life wasn't this backwater. His real life was business, and London, and his friends and family, and the beautiful, sophisticated women who passed through his bed without leaving a trace on his heart.

It was pure winter madness that right now only one woman's face lived in his memory. She was a slender redhead who was far too good for him.

Emilia nuzzled his back, and he realized he'd come to a dead stop in the blizzard. Even his thick wits recognized this was the surest way to ensure he never left this valley alive.

He took a swig of his godfather's brandy and patted his horse's snowy coat. "I'm sorry I dragged you out into this," he said through chattering teeth, as he slid the flask back into his pocket. He faced into the strengthening wind, which had veered around to blow straight toward him. "I had no choice."

But as he trudged ahead, making minuscule progress, he couldn't help remembering Maggie's stricken expression when he'd left. He'd nearly turned back at that moment, said to hell with honor. Joss Hale would recognize no law but the law of desire.

Was he out of his mind to struggle out here, when a mile behind him, Maggie waited? Warm. Welcoming. Beautiful.

Innocent. Unprotected. Gallant.

No, he couldn't ruin her for his own selfish pleasure. He wasn't such a cad, God blast it.

Joss gritted his teeth and narrowed his eyes against the flying snow. He pushed on and with every step, he battled to find some shred of compensation in doing the right thing, when wickedness was, oh, so tempting.

CHAPTER NINE

Maggie had fallen into a troubled doze in front of the fire when the door to the kitchens slammed open, letting a blast of freezing air inside.

Groggy and stiff with sitting still so long, she stumbled to her feet. Her sudden movement dislodged Smith, who jumped down from her lap and stalked off with her tail waving in displeasure.

"Joss…" she said, wondering if she was dreaming.

She hadn't really been asleep. Or at least she'd thought she wasn't.

Forbidden joy overwhelmed her. Then she looked at him more closely, and concern overcame every response but the need to help. "You look terrible."

He was utterly exhausted, with his eyes sunk back in his white face. Those deep lines between nose and mouth were like chasms.

Joss took a dragging step across the threshold, dropped his hat and saddlebags to the floor, and turned to fumble with the heavy old door. She rushed forward and slid her shoulder under his arm. He was freezing, shivering so violently that she had trouble holding onto him.

"I couldn't get through the pass." His voice was hoarse.

"Oh, my dear," she said, before she could think to censor herself.

He wasn't getting far with closing the door. She gave the heavy door a kick to shut it and helped him across the short distance to the hearth. Thank goodness the roaring fire kept the kitchens so warm.

Frantic, she tugged off his wet outdoor clothes and threw them to the floor. Her anxiety grew as he stood passively under her attentions. Joss Hale was many things, but passive wasn't one of them.

"God knows I tried," he said through chattering teeth. As the heat worked on him, he began to steam gently.

"I know you did," she said softly, pushing him onto the settle and going on her knees to tug off his icy boots.

And she did know. She suspected he'd tried far past the point where most men would have given up and turned back.

He was staring at her the way he'd stared at her when he first arrived. "You've been crying."

She must look a complete fright, but when he reached out and touched her cheek, she almost didn't mind. "Yes."

"I'm sorry, Maggie."

Sorry he'd left her and made her cry? Or sorry he came back? He looked too tired to meet emotional demands, although tomorrow they'd have to talk about what happened now. "How's Emilia?"

"I soon realized she wasn't likely to make it. If she was in a better state, I'd have done my best to go on."

Maggie's lips turned down in disapproval as she stood up. "Then you'd be a fool. This…feeling between us isn't worth dying for."

"Isn't it?"

"No," she snapped. She'd nearly lost him. To hide the queasy terror that thought aroused, she headed into the pantry to fetch some brandy. "Here. It will help."

As he accepted the bottle, he turned his face up toward her. Already some of the life came back into his features, but the hand that pulled out the cork was shaking. While he drank from the bottle, she went into the linen store.

When she emerged, carrying towels and blankets, he was slumped in the chair. The sag of his body expressed deathly weariness, and his long legs stretched toward the fire.

"Do you want me to dry your hair?" She might still sound angry, but the rusty taste of fear was sharp in her mouth. And guilt. How could she have let him go? She knew the dangers.

He raised his head to observe her brandishing a towel like a weapon. "No, thank you. I can manage."

The brandy and the fire had started to work their magic. That deep rumble of a voice almost sounded like usual. He reached out for the towel and began to wipe his neck and shoulders.

She didn't turn her eyes away when he stood to remove his coat. "Do you want to take off your breeches, too?"

"Why, Miss Carr, you make me blush," he said with an attempt at his usual humor.

"Don't make a joke of this, Joss." She whirled on him, wanting to fling herself into his arms and hold him forever. Wanting to punch him hard for putting himself in danger over something as insubstantial as honor. "You could have died."

"I'm sorry." With clumsy movements, he tugged off his shirt and let it fall to the floor. All urge to clout him evaporated, as did every drop of moisture in her mouth.

In the firelight, his chest was magnificent. Golden and powerful. Crisp black curls outlined his pectoral muscles and trailed down his flat belly to disappear beneath his leather breeches.

She bit her lip and stared at him wide-eyed. He limped close enough for her to smell the outdoors on his skin, and beneath that, the unforgettable essence of Joss himself.

"Don't be angry, sweetheart." His hand curled behind her neck, and he cupped the back of her head. "I'm safe."

She wasn't, and she knew it. But when he called her sweetheart, nothing could stop her sliding her arms around him. His skin was chilled, and she cuddled closer to share her warmth.

The intimacy of the embrace was extraordinary. She felt each breath he took and the subtle shift of muscles across his back, as he moved his hands up and down her spine in wordless comfort.

"You're a wild and reckless fool," she muttered into his chest.

He twined his arms around her. "I'm sorry I frightened you," he whispered, leaning his chin on her head. "I won't do it again."

"You'd better not," she said indistinctly, pressing her nose into his skin. As he warmed up, the glorious scent of Joss overpowered the scent of snow and wind.

"I promise."

The tenderness in that bass voice banished the last of her anger. Anger that was purely a reaction to overwhelming dread. If he'd died out there…

If ever Maggie had doubted how deeply her feelings for Joss Hale went, her quaking, unreasoning panic at the thought of losing him told her that she was in real trouble. When he'd left her, her world had turned cold and unwelcoming. But the idea of a world without him in it somewhere, even if far away, had been more than she could endure.

Inexplicable, illogical, unlikely, but she'd fallen desperately in love, and she had a grim premonition it was a lifelong affliction.

Still, she hadn't completely lost all connection with the mundane world. She stirred in Joss's arms and prepared to step away.

Joss tightened his hold to keep her close. "Where in blazes do you think you're going?"

"To put Emilia in the stables."

He didn't release her. "She's safely in her stall. I fed and watered her, and put a poultice on her leg before I came inside."

Maggie couldn't believe what she heard. "You looked after her when you were so close to collapsing?"

"My father taught me—care for yourself only after you've cared for your horse."

Her heart took a dizzying swoop, and she closed her eyes against a hot rush of tears. Curse him. What chance did she have against him?

She knew what state he was in, yet he'd seen his mount settled before he sought shelter and warmth for himself. "You're a good man, Josiah Hale."

He gave a grunt of self-derisive laughter. "No, by God, I'm not."

She knew he meant the words as a warning, but in her ears, they were a promise of sensual expertise.

Maggie met those deep-set eyes, and a quiver of need set up low in her stomach, until her whole body was shaking. Tonight, tomorrow, perhaps the day after, but soon, she'd give herself to this man. And words like sin and virtue, and right and wrong would have no power to stop her.

Because her fate opened up before her, for good or ill, she was content to postpone the difficult decisions that lay ahead. "What about your breeches?"

He was wise enough not to tease her this time. "The leather keeps the water out."

His arms tightened, before abruptly he staggered away. She wasn't feeling too solid either. Standing on her own two feet had her struggling to lock rubbery knees. The rush of blood to her head left her giddy and disconcerted.

Because touching his naked skin hadn't been entirely about comfort and shared warmth. How could it be? Maggie wanted this man, and she knew he wanted her. As the effects of his ordeal wore off, she'd noticed how he responded to her nearness.

She touched him because she wanted to. She touched him for desire. For pleasure.

For...love.

But her first priority now was to look after him. While it was a pity to cover up that superb torso, she passed him a blanket. "I should never have sent you away."

"You didn't send me away. I went." The straight look

he shot her threatened to upset her wanton plans. When he wrapped the blanket around his shoulders, he looked like a dashing Roman. "We need to talk."

"Not now." Avoiding that searching green gaze, she scooped up the wet shirt he'd discarded and bundled it near the fire. If she washed it after supper and hung it before the hearth, it would dry overnight. "Warm up. Eat. Rest. We'll talk later."

And perhaps they wouldn't.

Another shiver rippled through her. This time alive with anticipation.

"Maggie—"

"Sit near the fire while I heat up some of yesterday's soup." She gestured to the stove. "You'll be hungry."

She was hungry, too. Odd to think that not long ago, she'd felt like she never wanted to eat again. What a range of emotions the day had brought. Joy. Passion. Guilt. Sorrow. Despair. Fear.

To her surprise, he obeyed without an argument. Sign enough that he was still in a bad way. She beat back her fear and concentrated on her cooking. When she glanced across to where he slouched on the settle, she was glad to see his eyes closed. Sleep was what he needed after what he'd been through.

When the meal was ready, she crossed to shake his shoulder. "Joss, wake up."

The smile he gave her was so sweet, she almost took him in her arms. But right now, he needed food more than he needed her embrace. "Sorry. I dozed off."

"Have something to eat, then go to bed." When she took his hand, it was no longer icy cold. She blinked away hot tears of relief.

Maggie helped him across to the table she'd set, watching his halting progress with a frown. He was still moving with arthritic stiffness. With a groan, he collapsed into the chair.

Knowing he wasn't yet up to much conversation, she didn't try to talk to him as they started eating. Only once he'd made short work of his soup and she saw some color return to his face, did she speak. "Tell me what happened," she said, putting down her spoon.

"You were right. I left my departure too late." He hitched up his blanket and leaned back in his chair, half-full wineglass in one hand. "It started snowing as soon as I got to the end of the drive."

"You should have turned back at that point."

He still sounded mortally tired. "You know why I didn't."

Maggie did. She cut him a huge wedge of the beef pie she'd warmed in the oven and slid it onto his plate. She'd looked after his meals since he'd arrived. Tonight why did this basic act of hospitality seem particularly… wifely? "Had Emilia started limping by then?"

"No. And I only had a few miles to go."

"It must have been so frightening. I've been caught in a snowstorm a couple of times. I completely lost my sense of direction."

"I could still make out the shape of the hills. And the

prevailing wind has been from the north since I arrived. I wasn't likely to get lost."

She was overjoyed to hear him sounding much more like himself. "You noticed that?"

He shrugged and began to eat once more. "An architect notes a house's cold and warm spots. Whoever built Thorncroft knew what they were doing. A small difference in the windows and the doors, and the place would be freezing."

"It's usually a warm house," she said, serving herself a smaller piece of pie. "Especially with all the fires lit."

Yet how cold and forbidding it had felt after Joss left. Now, it was the Garden of Eden. Such a difference love could make.

"We got to the pass, but it was blocked. I tried to go over the hills and around, but that proved impossible, too."

Maggie could imagine how he'd struggled on. When he left her, she'd seen his determination. And regret.

She began to eat her pie. "I'm glad you had the good sense to come back."

He sent her a hard look. "Are you?"

Joss had demolished his pie, too, so she served him the rest. "I don't want you lying dead and frozen on a hillside."

"That's nice to know," he said, with a hint of his familiar dryness.

He looked much better already. Remarkable, really, how quickly he recovered. It gave her hope that he mightn't suffer any long-term effects from his trials.

She matched his tone. "Once the spring thaws start, the shepherds get upset if they find travelers who didn't make it through the snow."

When humor lightened Joss's features, her heart cramped with helpless love. "By all means, let's keep the shepherds happy."

Joss took Maggie's advice and retired to his room early. He'd done his best to hide quite how battered he felt after fighting the elements, but his body ached like the devil from that long tramp hauling a lame horse. He'd been in a damned bad way when he'd staggered back to Thorncroft Hall.

He'd thought winters in Sussex could be grim. He'd had no idea how bitter cold weather could be until he struck these wild northern uplands.

Now he lay in his big, warm bed, and knew he couldn't entirely blame his restlessness on the aftereffects of his ordeal. Unsatisfied desire proved more agonizing by far than mere aches and pains.

Since he'd arrived at Thorncroft, he'd spent hours lying awake in his room, hungering for Maggie. But tonight the yearning was sharper, more focused. Now he knew how her kisses tasted, and how perfectly she fitted in his arms, and the sounds she made when she enjoyed a man's attentions.

Tonight he knew she wanted him, too.

Nothing had changed since he'd headed out on his futile quest to reach Little Flitwick. It was still wrong to seduce Maggie. Of course it was. Otherwise he wouldn't have embarked on a journey that brought him to the brink of disaster.

But wrong or not, dear God, how he longed to have her here beside him. How he burned to see her all warm and rosy and responsive, the way she'd been after his kisses beside the pond.

The girl he'd first met had had sad eyes. But she hadn't been sad when they'd skated, and when they'd kissed, and tonight when she'd welcomed him back. She'd been incandescent with joy.

And he'd recognized then that their coming together was inevitable. From the first moment, she'd caught him in her spell. Was that only four days ago?

He felt like he'd lived through a lifetime since.

Joss closed his eyes and surrendered to exhaustion, dreaming of Maggie becoming his at last.

The sound of the door opening pierced Joss's dreams of fighting to reach Maggie through snow as sticky as melted wax. Instantly alert, he opened his eyes. He felt no disorientation. He knew where he was. He knew who had come in, even before he rolled over to face the doorway.

Elation surged so powerfully, it was painful. His heart began to race, and his mouth went dry with anticipation. He must have been asleep a couple of hours. The fire burned low and painted the chamber dull gold.

"Maggie?"

The woman who was his delight and his torment hovered on the threshold. Her hand shook so badly that her candle sent shadows jumping against the walls. She wore the white flannel nightdress, familiar from his first night.

Joss knew better than to take her presence for granted. Her arrival mightn't mean what he so desperately hoped it did. "Are you in trouble?"

"Yes…" Her voice was a frail thread.

He was out of bed before he recalled he was naked and that if she'd come to ask for help, a huge lummox wearing nothing but his skin was likely to scare her silly. "What's wrong?"

Her eyes, dark and mysterious, widened as she stared at his body. The candlelight performed a slow waltz. Joss saw her delicate throat move as she swallowed.

"I'm sorry," he said gruffly, fumbling to find his dressing gown. Until he remembered it was in his pack. He'd been so bloody tired and sore when he came upstairs, he'd toppled straight into bed.

Her attention fell to where his cock rose hard and insistent against his belly. Through the uncertain light, he saw a delicious wash of pink color her cheeks. The dangers of sharing this house with her had never been so starkly apparent as they were right now.

When she lifted her eyes, he couldn't mistake the desire he saw in her face. She licked her lips as if she wanted to taste him, the way a hungry man wanted to dive into eating an extravagant meal. Even through his astonishment, his body reacted predictably.

"Don't be sorry."

That whisper played havoc with his control. With difficulty, he resisted the urge to cover himself like a bashful schoolboy. Instead he turned away and walked across to where his saddlebags rested against the wall.

She'd get an eyeful of his bare arse, but damn it, what choice did he have? His hands weren't much steadier than hers when he opened his bag and rooted out his dressing gown. He shrugged it on, worried that Maggie remained so deathly quiet.

Even though he could no longer see her, her image burned in his brain. Slender. Graceful body wreathed in white, as incendiary a sight as a blatantly naked courtesan. Her auburn plait curled across her breast, following the path that his hands itched to trace.

Battling for control, he turned as he tied the sash. She was staring at him as if she beheld the wonder of the ages. That did nothing to cool his arousal. The beat of blood in his head was so loud, he had trouble hearing her.

"I forget how…big you are. And then…"

Then he started prancing around with his tackle waving in the breeze. Maggie Carr was the one woman in creation who could make him blush. How his louche chums in London would cackle to see libertine Joss Hale turn as awkward as a boy with his first lass.

And all because that lass was so breathtakingly beautiful.

And fragile.

And strong.

All his tried and true strategies with a pretty girl seemed tired and outmoded. Because never before had his heart been involved in a seduction.

He wasn't a fool. Nor was he in the habit of deceiving himself. From the first, Maggie had stirred something more profound than a young man's natural yen to bed a comely wench.

But only now did he realize how close he came to loving her. Whatever happened tonight—whatever happened after tonight—this affair would change him forever.

"Then I see how huge you are."

Joss knew she described his size as a whole, but all this talk about dimensions made his dick swell with excitement. Yet the possibility remained that he was getting all worked up about nothing.

"You said you need my help."

She squared her shoulders as if facing some great task. "I do."

His stomach dropped. Disappointment made his voice crack. Disappointment he had no right to feel, damn it. "Are you ill?"

To his surprise, Maggie took a faltering step into the room. Even as he counseled caution, his heart turned a somersault. She must realize that entering his territory was dangerous.

"No, I'm not ill." Maggie shifted from one bare foot to the other. She had to be freezing. But unlike their first night, he didn't trust himself to lay his hands on her.

"Then what is it?" He cursed the impatience in his voice, but having her so near in this silent house asked too much of a mere mortal.

The stillness somehow worsened his torture. When he'd gone to bed, the wind had been howling like the hounds of hell, but it had since dropped. He felt like the world held its breath to see what happened next, and every word he and Maggie spoke carried the weight of destiny.

She bit her lip, and he closed his eyes against the sight of small white teeth sinking into cushiony pink flesh. He rapidly reached a point where if she didn't leave, he wouldn't be responsible for the consequences. He wanted her so badly, each breath hurt.

"I…I could have lost you today." Her voice was low and husky. "You tried to make light of it, but you forget

I live here, and I know the risks you took when you went."

"I know the risks if I stay here." His voice rasped. "You're a chaste woman."

"Yes, I am." She grimaced. "But what use is that chastity to me?"

This time, the silence crashed down as hard as an avalanche. Before he could stop himself, Joss stepped closer. He spoke through a tight throat. "You're not thinking clearly. You're upset because I got caught in the snow. In the morning, you'll regret any rash decision."

Why in Hades did he try to talk her out of yielding, when it was so bloody obvious that was what they both wanted? But for the first time in what he recognized as a selfish life, his pleasure wasn't of paramount importance.

"I am thinking clearly." A stubborn expression settled on her face, banished her nervousness. "Until you came, my life was flat and meaningless. Each day was exactly the same as the last. Once you leave, that's what my life will go back to."

The bleak picture she painted made his gut knot with pity. A pity he knew she'd despise. "Sweetheart—"

Her voice hardened as she ventured closer, until only a few feet separated them. "In the years to come, when the nights are cold and the bed is too big for one person, I want something glorious to remember. Don't make me beg, Joss."

For pity's sake, what could he do, when she said that? He knew what was right, but he needed her so desperately.

"Come here, Maggie."

The tension drained from her expression, and she launched forward. The sudden movement did for the candle, and it flickered out as Joss's arms closed hard around soft flannel and softer woman.

CHAPTER TEN

irelit night descended like a benediction. With a luxuriant sigh, Maggie melted against Joss as he bent his ruffled head to kiss her. The snuffed candle fell to the ground with a soft thud, while she kissed him back with all the longing in her heart.

The flickering, concealing darkness was welcome. It saved her blushes. Because while she came to Joss with no regrets, enough of the vicar's daughter remained for shyness to set its claws into her.

She knew now how to tease and lure and play, so their kisses quickly turned into a passionate game. After a brief, fumbling moment, he whipped the night-dress over her head and cast it away.

Fleeting self-consciousness cramped her stomach. She'd never been naked with a man before. But the heat of Joss's lips against hers soon blasted any bashfulness to ashes.

His hands explored bare skin, tracing searing trails wherever he touched. He kissed an incendiary line down her neck, making her shiver and gasp. His hands found her breasts, and he played with her nipples until they were hard and aching. A powerful pulse set up between her legs. On an incoherent plea, she pressed closer, shoving the edges of his dressing gown aside.

Shocked pleasure punched the breath from her lungs, when she felt his hardness rising against her stomach. The darkness encouraged her boldness, although she couldn't help remembering how huge and demanding he'd looked when he left the bed. She shivered with a heady mixture of trepidation and excitement.

Maggie sucked air into her starved lungs. He smelled like heaven. Surely she could live on his scent alone. She rubbed her face against him, feeling the soft friction of hair against her cheek.

"May I touch you?" she murmured into his skin.

"Oh, yes," he groaned, nipping at the curve of her shoulder.

Grateful that the banked fire left her in shadow, she pulled far enough away to untie the dressing gown. Her hands were clumsy, and by the time she'd released the knot, they were both panting with impatience. She pushed the heavy garment from his shoulders. With a rustle, it fell to the floor.

Tentative hands fluttered up his arms and down his

chest. She'd touched his chest before, but now every caress brought her nearer to their union.

"You're so warm."

He caught her hand and pressed it to where his heart hammered against his ribs. "Let me keep you warm."

What an irresistible offer. Until he came to Thorncroft, her life had been endlessly cold.

"Yes," she whispered, leaning in to kiss one firm male pectoral.

The room's dusky light brought senses other than sight to the fore. His scent hung rich in the air. His skin was smooth beneath her hands, and tasted of salt and snow. His breath was an erratic rasp in her ears.

"Let me undo your hair." Joss shivered under her kiss and spread his hand across the back of her head, holding her face against him. He nuzzled her temple. "I've dreamed about seeing your hair loose around your shoulders."

"Have you?" Maggie asked in surprise.

His low groan was a growl against her ear. "Good God, yes."

Wonder flooded her, and she felt like she dissolved into a warm puddle of honey. He'd dreamed of her. How amazing. Perhaps they were more equal in this desire than she'd imagined. "I had no idea."

"Don't you know you've haunted my every thought, since the moment I stumbled over the threshold and fell into the clutches of a cranky fairy?"

With a choked laugh, she pressed another kiss to his chest. "That doesn't sound very appealing."

His lips drifted down, and he nipped her earlobe between his teeth. The sting set desire churning in her belly and jammed the breath in her throat. Her fingers encircled the firm flesh of his arms, as she fought to keep her balance under the overwhelming onslaught of sensation.

"A sweet, exquisite fairy."

"That's better." She'd arrived at his door in a grim spirit of necessity. Joss, bless him, showed her that starlight shone through the darkness.

"I've had a million fantasies about your beautiful hair."

She straightened and stared up at him. When he smiled, she caught the gleam of his eyes. "You make me so happy."

He cradled her head between his hands and kissed her. "And I've hardly started."

"Undo my hair," Maggie said, amazed at the way such a seemingly innocuous act became so significant, once she stood naked before the man she wanted. When he reached out and with a shaking hand untied the ribbon, she felt like she presented him with a precious gift.

They stood so close, she heard the hitch in his breath when he began to part the strands. She trembled under his touch. As his hands moved, his knuckles brushed her breasts, setting off a cascade of thrills.

It took him forever to unbind her hair, but some instinct held her back from helping. At last she felt the soft tickle of hair across her naked skin.

With a reverent touch, he began to run his fingers through her long hair. His deep sigh of satisfaction communicated his pleasure in her in a way mere words never could.

"Lovely," he murmured, lifting a silky hank and letting it drift down through his fingers so it caught the red glow of the firelight. "Lovely, lovely, lovely."

Confidence unfurled in her heart. Joss wanted her. She already knew that, of course. But she hadn't known he dreamed of her. She hadn't known he yearned the way she'd yearned.

Her hair cascaded in thick auburn waves down to her waist. With another of those wordless sounds of appreciation, Joss collected great handfuls and buried his face in it. She smiled, enjoying his pleasure, and stroked his head, the crisp curls cool under her fingers.

"Let me light the candles," he said urgently as he raised his head. "I need to see you."

"Next time," she whispered, feeling daring and wanton as she thought of the nights stretching ahead of them.

White teeth glinted as he smiled. "Yes, next time."

He swung her up into his arms, so she felt like she was flying, the way she'd felt like she was flying when they skated. With Joss, her soul took wing.

Helpless against the wild clamor of desire, she

curved into his body and slid one arm around his powerful neck. "I love how strong you are."

I love you.

That rumble of subterranean amusement always made her heart skip a beat. "I'm a big brute, that's for sure."

"You can pick me up with one hand," she said breathlessly.

"Not quite." He laughed softly. "How angry you were when I hauled you down to the kitchens that first night. I thought my boldness must bring a fairy curse down on my head."

She buried her nose in his neck, inhaling his essence as if she tested a fine wine. "I feel magical tonight."

His hold tightened. "You've always been magical."

If only she did have mystical powers. She'd wave her wand and keep Joss captive forever. "I've forgiven you for treating me like a sack of potatoes."

"I should hope so, after I did all that hard work with the Christmas decorations. I've been your beast of burden ever since I arrived. I thought you'd never finish ordering me around when we were cutting the greenery."

She gave the hair at his nape a sharp tug, loving that he teased her. "You enjoyed it."

Since she'd lost her mother, nobody had teased her. Growing up in the vicarage in Kent, Maggie had learned that laughter was an essential part of love.

Laughter had been largely absent during her last five years at Thorncroft.

Until Joss arrived. He'd given her so many gifts, not just the gift of this glorious passion burning bright between them.

"I was cold and wet, and under orders from an otherworldly being."

She tugged his hair again. "So?"

"So I did indeed enjoy it. I said you have magic, Maggie."

"I hope so." Loving the subtle slide of her skin upon his, she laid her head on his bare shoulder.

"Shall we make magic together now?" His voice was low and serious.

When she nodded her head, her cheek caressed his arm in a silent declaration of love. "Don't make me wait any longer."

Gently Joss set Maggie on the bed and came down over her. How natural all this seemed. As if ordained to happen. He felt no guilt—although seducing an innocent went against every principle—just an overwhelming gratitude that he'd discovered her. It would have been so easy to bypass this unforgettable woman, hidden in this secret, snowy dale.

Questions of servant and master didn't matter. Had

never mattered, despite her absurd and charming attempts to keep to her place when he first arrived.

Now Maggie Carr was in his bed. What a marvelous outcome. He dedicated himself to exciting her, learning the places on her body that gave her pleasure. He scraped his teeth across her neck until she shivered in helpless response. His hands traced her breasts and hips and arms, the hollow of her navel, the sensitive skin behind her knees, the luscious curve of her buttocks. Her muffled gasps of surprise and delight were a symphony in his ears, sweeter than any music he'd ever heard.

"You're so soft," he said in appreciation, as his hand curled around one perfect breast.

An exhalation of amusement greeted his statement. "And you're so hard."

She was astonishing. He gave a bark of laughter and caught her hand, pressing it to his cock.

"Oh, Lord…" she breathed in awe.

"Touch me."

"I don't know what to do."

"Like this."

Tensing every muscle against spilling into her fist, he arranged her trembling fingers around him. Her hesitant exploration sizzled through him like lightning. Battling for control, he buried his face in her shoulder and inhaled the humid scent of her skin.

Without his encouragement, her grip tightened.

The jolt of arousal nearly blew the top of his head off, and his jaw set so rigid, it ached.

"Joss, are you all right?" Her other hand curved across his back, stroking him.

"Yes," he said in a strangled voice.

"You don't sound all right," she said doubtfully.

That rhythmic stroking threatened to send him over the edge. He felt torn between pleasure and pain, but when she began to withdraw her hand from between his legs, he caught her and brought her back.

"Don't stop," he growled, lifting his head and trying to make out her expression through the gloom. Her spiky breathing betrayed rising excitement.

She moved her hand up and down his length, squeezing as she went. It was exquisite. It was vilest torture.

"How the…devil do you know to do that?"

Maggie stretched up to kiss his lips. The melting sweetness of the kiss contrasted with her greedy hands on his erect prick. "I wondered if you might like it. I like it when you stroke me."

"Keep going…" he groaned, closing his eyes and letting her find her way.

She was clumsy. She was breathtaking. She turned his world upside down.

And eventually he had to stop her. Because he needed to be inside her more than he needed the hope of heaven. He placed one hand over hers. "It's my turn to drive you mad."

When he shifted to his side, she spread before him like a banquet. He wished he could see every superb inch. But he was wise enough to know that in full light, his Maggie would likely prove shy, instead of happy to play the seducer.

As she'd said with such heart-stopping naturalness, there was next time.

The large bed remained mostly in shadow, but when she moved, he caught a tantalizing glimpse of her body. More impression than detail. Round breasts tipped with beaded nipples. The slender line of her thighs. The dip of her stomach.

His hand drifted down over her breasts, lingering to tease until she was moaning and shifting against the sheets.

"You are driving me mad," she said unsteadily.

Smiling, he raised his head. "That's the general idea."

He took her nipple between his lips, scraping his teeth over the sensitive tip. She shuddered, and a cry of startled pleasure escaped her. "That feels so wicked."

"But nice."

Her fingers tangled in his hair and brought him back to her breast. "Definitely nice."

Joss smiled against her softness. He drew on her nipple, while his palm traced random circles over her stomach. On each pass, he ventured lower, until his fingers tangled in the feathery hair above her sex. With every second, he fell deeper into her mystery.

And a tantalizing mystery indeed were the secrets between her thighs. "Part your legs for me, Maggie," he murmured.

She obeyed unquestioningly. Her trust sliced through him like a sword.

He leaned back on his elbow to watch her. His eyes had adjusted to the low light, so he made out her features and the sumptuous spill of her spectacular hair across the pillows.

Slowly, using the delay to build his anticipation, he slid his hand down until he touched her cleft. She made a faint, startled sound as he stroked her sleekness. His thumb brushed the center of her pleasure, and she made another sound deep in her throat. She reached to catch his arm.

"Don't you like it?"

"It's…odd," she said in a choked voice. "Do you like it?"

Testing her arousal and finding her ready for him? Luring her along the path to pleasure? "Oh, yes," he sighed, tracing a small circle around the pearl of flesh. "Trust me."

"I do," she said shakily. If her actions hadn't proven beyond question that she did, he might doubt her. "This is…more than I expected."

"That's good, isn't it?"

The inhibiting hand still encircled his arm. "I suppose so."

"You don't sound very sure."

"I'm not."

A disagreeable thought struck him, and he wondered if he went too fast after all. "You know what's going to happen?"

"In theory," she muttered, kneading his biceps in a nervous rhythm. "My mother told me. She didn't believe in keeping girls ignorant."

Relief filled him. "Good for your mother."

"But she didn't tell me about…this."

Caressing her, he pressed his lips to hers. At first she was distracted, but she swiftly got into the spirit and relaxed against the sheets. At last she released his arm, and her hand drifted down to drape across her stomach.

Slowly he pulled away, taking her lower lip in his teeth and biting down gently. Before she could start worrying about what came next, he slid a finger inside her.

Maggie was deliciously tight and slick. When he curled his finger against the walls of her passage and moved it in and out, a sumptuous liquid surge greeted him.

"Oh…" she said in audible shock.

"You're perfect," he said softly, bending to suckle one nipple. The pressure at her breast made her clench against his seeking finger, and she rewarded him with another of those quivery exhalations that sounded gloriously like the beginnings of pleasure.

How he loved to hear her discover her capacity for

sensual delight. She laid her hand on his chest, where his heart galloped fit to burst. When she was sighing with every stroke, Joss eased two fingers into her, relishing her body's welcome.

The scent of her need hung heavy on the still air. He licked his lips, longing to taste her.

Something else for next time. Her quick response and the sweet sounds of her enjoyment pushed him to a point where he could wait no longer.

He rolled over her, pleased that she instinctively moved to cradle him between her thighs. Her arms slid around his back, and she gazed up at him through the flickering light. Her blue eyes were dark and gleaming, and her kiss-swollen lips parted over small white teeth.

Joss stared down into her vivid face. Despite his urgency, he paused. At this, the zenith of desire, he recognized this moment's life-changing importance.

He'd always been restless. Eager for the next challenge. Sharing this bed with Maggie Carr, he felt anchored for the first time. As if all his seeking found a purpose he'd never realized was lacking.

She was his home.

Joss kissed her with a reverence that was almost holy, even as he tightened his hips and pressed into her body.

CHAPTER ELEVEN

Maggie bit her lips, as the pressure between her legs verged toward the edge of pain.

Above her, Joss was hard and huge. He was breathing in great noisy gusts, and beneath her hands, the muscles of his back were as unyielding as rock. As unyielding as that part of him invading her body.

When he moved a fraction deeper, she couldn't muffle a whimper. Immediately he stopped and rose on his elbows to stare down at her through the flame-tinged darkness. "My darling, I'm sorry."

He sounded like the Joss she knew, like the Joss she loved. She sucked a breath into starved lungs, and her discomfort faded a fraction.

She lifted one hand to caress his stubborn jaw. "I like you calling me your darling."

"Is it so bad?"

He sounded in such torment at the thought of hurting her that she almost forgot her pain. "I can bear it."

"I'll be careful." He reached down and hooked her knees up. The strain eased.

"I like being so close to you."

This closeness, she knew, could well result in a child. She'd faced that possibility before she'd come to him and decided that she was willing to take the risk.

"I'll get closer yet." He kissed her with all the passion she sensed he was reining in so he didn't hurt her.

Maggie closed her eyes and gave herself up to the pleasure of his lips on hers, so when he plunged forward and claimed her, the pain hardly registered.

He raised his head. "Are you all right?"

Better than that. Much better. She felt filled and possessed and united with Joss. Despite the shaky beginning, she found herself smiling. "Yes. Yes, I am."

She slid her bottom further down in the bed, and the angle of Joss's penetration changed delightfully. At last she started to notice things, apart from the strangeness of a man's body joined with hers. How his warmth radiated into her. How she felt his every breath. How his scent marked the air—and her.

"There's more."

She ran her hand down his face, whiskers prickling

under her palm, and set it on his broad shoulder. "Show me."

Slowly he withdrew. She braced for discomfort, but the long glide set every nerve in her body singing.

"Oh," she said, astounded at the revival of the glorious responses she'd experienced when he'd first touched her. She'd imagined such pleasure belonged purely to the prelude. Most wonderfully, it seemed that she was wrong.

Even more wonderful, he paused and thrust again, pushing her deep into the mattress. This time the sensation of being taken over was wholly rapturous.

"Oh, Joss," she sighed.

When he kissed her, the sweep of his tongue into her mouth had her squeezing around him. He groaned against her lips. "Good God above, do that again."

"This?"

His answer was a long, jagged sigh. "You're made for delight, Maggie." He paused. "You're made for me."

Before she could question that hoarse statement, he started to move more purposefully, stealing all capacity for speech. But something in that husky bass declaration had sounded like love. And her last misgivings fled.

Because she had been made for him. Just as he was made for her.

He settled into a hard, driving rhythm that sparked a spiraling, craving sensation inside her. Blindly she tilted her hips to meet him, seeking relief from the surging need. But still the tension built, until her breath emerged in harsh sobs. Surely if this went on, she must shatter into a million pieces.

Joss rose above her, and she felt he went so deep into her body, he became part of her. She released a choked moan and tightened her grip on his hard male shoulders as he drove her higher.

He slipped a shaking hand between her legs and touched her in that place that made her tremble. A blast of exquisite sensation seized her, and on a flash of blinding light, she tumbled over into the abyss.

But the abyss was bright and hot, and she was safe in her lover's arms, even as she soared through space, slicing through the flames like an eagle.

In the midst of transfiguring joy, she heard Joss give a long, guttural groan. As he plunged inside her, the sinews under her hands tightened. A rush of heat flooded her womb. As she drifted through sublime heights, she felt him pump into her.

He groaned again and slumped down, forcing the breath out of her. Maggie didn't mind. She'd imagined she couldn't feel closer to him than she had in those transcendent, transforming moments at her peak. But now with him collapsed over her in exhaustion, their bodies still joined, she felt a richer, deeper union with this man she loved.

His head was buried in the curve of her neck, and he was shaking. She tangled her fingers in the damp curls at his nape and smiled up into the shadows, her mind full of what had happened between them.

She'd satisfied him. Even in her inexperience, she knew that. And in return, he'd shown her a world beyond her wildest imaginings.

Eventually he shifted, and Maggie sucked in her first full breath in what felt like forever. He rose above her, his face in shadow. "You're a miracle, Margaret Carr. I never want to be apart from you again."

"Joss?" she asked, more shocked by what he said than by what they'd just done, extraordinary and magnificent as that had been.

Instead of answering her, he kissed her again. She waited for more passion, but Joss's lips expressed tenderness, verging on worship.

When he lifted his head, she was trembling. In the uncertain light, those dark green eyes seemed to send her a message too profound for mere words. "Wait here."

She frowned, caught by surprise.

Wait here? What on earth was happening?

"What's wrong?"

"Absolutely nothing, my darling." He cupped her jaw in his hand. "But I have something important to talk about, and I want to do it right."

After another brief kiss, he rolled out of bed and found his dressing gown. More slowly, Maggie sat up and pulled the sheets over her bare breasts. His unexpected behavior was making her self-conscious, as she hadn't been since she'd offered herself to him.

Movement set up a myriad of twinges in her secret places, reminders of the marvelous things Joss had done to her. The skin on her cheeks, neck and breasts stung. During their turbulent passion, his whiskers had chafed her.

"Why can't we stay here?"

She caught the flash of white teeth as he smiled. "Trust me."

He'd said that before he claimed her body.

Well, that had worked out fine, hadn't it? She told herself to have faith.

Joss stepped closer and kissed her with more of that soul-searching tenderness. She'd basked in his passion, but this sweetness left her completely defenseless. Reminded her that while he'd given her so much, he hadn't given her the promises her aching heart longed for.

Maggie reminded herself that she hadn't asked for promises. When she'd arrived at his door, she'd just been desperate to give herself to the man she loved. The man who could so easily be lying frozen and dead out on the hills tonight, instead of standing beside the bed, teasing her.

But now that she knew what joy they created together, the prospect of Joss moving on and perhaps forgetting her was unbearable. Life had taught her not to be greedy, but when she looked at her bold and vital lover, she felt greedy.

For more pleasure. For more life.

For more...him.

She'd hoped that satisfying her desire would provide memories to compensate for the years of loneliness ahead. But watching Joss as he left the room—a foretaste of his final departure—she realized she'd made a fundamental and catastrophic mistake.

Because one night wasn't enough. Even if he stayed until Jane came back, it wouldn't be enough.

When a woman loved a man as much as Maggie loved Joss, a whole lifetime wasn't enough.

The day he rode away from Thorncroft, he'd leave her life in ruins. And it was too late to do anything to save herself from the coming devastation.

The light from Joss's candelabra disturbed Maggie's troubled sleep. She hadn't heard him return—he really did move like a cat.

She blinked and yawned. Her forebodings about the future hadn't kept her awake. She was exhausted after a day of life-changing events and emotional upheaval. Not to mention those energetic hours skating in the cold, fresh air.

"Joss?" she asked sleepily, rolling onto her side so she could see him standing in the doorway. In his crimson velvet robe, he looked tall and oddly exotic, like a pasha visiting the harem to choose a concubine for a night's pleasure. "Is everything all right?"

"More than all right."

This was the first chance she'd had to see him properly since her candle had flickered out, all those tumultuous hours ago. He looked younger. And happy. And free from the burden of what she now recognized as unsatisfied desire. She only noted the signs of his tension by their absence. A tightness around his eyes and jaw. A rigid straightness of the shoulders. A certain care with how he moved.

Now Joss looked like a man at ease in his world in a way he hadn't since his arrival. How glad Maggie was to know that he'd found joy in her arms.

She pushed the blankets aside and slid over to make room for him. One thing she'd promised herself before she closed her eyes—she wasn't going to spoil current happiness with fretting about future misery. "Come back to bed."

"That's a tempting invitation."

"I hope so."

He strode forward and set her shawl on the bed beside her and her slippers on the floor. Her heart had leaped so high at the sight of him that she hadn't noticed what he carried.

"First, I'd like you to come downstairs. I've got something to say, and my bedroom isn't the right venue."

She frowned, although she sat up and swung her

feet to the ground, grateful that she was respectably covered. Before falling asleep, she'd tugged her nightdress over her nakedness. Without Joss's incendiary presence, she'd felt awkward, lying in his bed without a stitch to cover her.

"You're being very mysterious."

If she hadn't seen his happiness, if he hadn't told her she was a miracle, she might fear that he meant to say their liaison couldn't continue. But when he'd opened his arms to her, he also opened the doors of his soul. Now he was being tantalizingly enigmatic, but she didn't sense any withdrawal from their essential closeness.

"Aren't I just?" He dropped to his knees in front of her. She smiled to see the tangled mess of thick black curls, as he bent his head to his task. Her Joss would never be a neat, conventional man. "Let me help you with your slippers. I'd hate your feet to get cold."

All impulse to laughter evaporated. Maggie gulped back the emotion that surged to jam her throat. Nobody had looked after her in years. Yet Joss had cared for her from the first. Odd to think back to how angry she'd been when he'd carried her down to the kitchens that first night.

"I can manage."

"Let me." He slid her slippers onto her feet.

"You're smiling." She reached out to touch the groove of amusement creasing his cheek.

The fondness in his smile reassured her further.

He'd asked her to trust him. It was too late to start building defensive walls.

"I was thinking if you only knew how frequently white flannel has featured in my fantasies since we met."

A low laugh escaped her. "I'm sorry I didn't come to you in silk and satin."

"I'm not. I'm just glad you came to me at all. You make me so happy, Maggie."

"And you make me happy, Joss," she whispered.

At that moment it was true. What ensued in the coming weeks, months, years had no power to destroy her current pleasure in his presence.

With a gentleness that made tears prick her eyes—dear heaven, she threatened to become a watering pot—he lifted one foot and placed a kiss on her instep. The sensation of his lips on her skin made the deepest parts of her body heat and soften.

Joss raised his head and smiled again. She'd always loved his smile. She loved the way it added flashing charm to his rugged features.

When they'd first met, she'd thought him appealing, if not exactly handsome. Tonight, after nearly a week in his company, she thought him the most attractive man she'd ever met. She wouldn't trade an inch of that rugged, quirky, interesting face for the greatest beau in the kingdom.

"Don't look at me like that, or I'll forget good intentions."

She smiled back. "I like it when you forget good intentions."

His grip on her foot tightened. "So do I."

To her regret, he replaced her foot on the floor and rose. He lifted the candelabra and stretched out his hand. "Come with me."

Wrapping her shawl around her shoulders, she stood. "Won't you tell me what this is about?"

"Don't you like surprises?"

She curled her fingers around his. "I do, if they're nice surprises."

"I think this will count as a nice surprise."

Curiosity ate at her, as they left his room and followed the corridor to the staircase. After the storms, it seemed deathly quiet. The candlelight flickered against the high walls, picking out a distant building in a landscape painting or the gleam of a painted eye in a portrait.

Maggie shivered. She wasn't particularly superstitious, but she felt like a thousand ghosts gathered to observe their progress. Away from the fire, the house was freezing, and she moved closer to Joss. His big body radiated heat like a great furnace.

"I hope we're not going far."

"Now that's interesting." His grip on her hand firmed. "I'm hoping we'll go very far indeed."

She frowned. Was he talking about her sensual education? Or something more permanent? He'd said he never wanted to part from her. Did he mean to ask her to return to London as his mistress? But surely he must know that was a step too far, even for a woman who tonight had cast her bonnet over a windmill.

Before Maggie summoned the nerve to ask what he meant, they stopped outside the drawing room. Joss released her to place his hand on the door and look down at her with an unreadable expression. "Do you know it's Christmas Eve?"

Puzzled she met his gaze. "I suppose so."

It must be well after midnight, so of course it was Christmas Eve. As if to confirm the fact, the long clock in the hall chimed three.

"Christmas Eve is a magical time. A time when wishes come true."

"I've never heard that," she said skeptically, used by now to the charming nonsense he spouted about Christmas.

Although he could be right about the magic, because this was the first Christmas since her mother died when she'd derived an ounce of joy from the season. All because of Joss.

"Yes, you have. Don't children go to bed on Christmas Eve, dreaming of presents and all the fun and games to come the next day?"

It was a long time since she'd had such a Christmas Eve. "I'm not a child anymore."

"Everyone's a child at Christmas." He leaned in to kiss her briefly, setting off a cascade of pleasure. Would she ever take these spontaneous expressions of affection for granted? "Come with me."

He pushed the door open to a blaze of light. Maggie halted on the threshold, lost in wonder.

Joss must have unearthed every candle in the house. Flickering lights ranged across the mantel above the fire blazing in the hearth. Branches of candles covered every table. Combined with the Christmas greenery they'd had such a lovely time putting up, the effect was like a bower in an enchanted forest.

He stepped inside the room, and she followed in a daze of love and gratitude. Her shawl slipped to the ground, but the room was so cozy, it hardly mattered.

"Joss, this is lovely," she said, touched that he'd taken this trouble for her.

He strode into the center of the floor, where he'd arranged a circle of fat beeswax candles, all burning bravely against the dark winter night. "Aren't you glad we got the house ready for Christmas?"

Before his arrival, how lonely and closed away she'd been. Christmas had meant nothing to her. But right now, her heart was so full of love and gratitude, she felt like that dismal girl was another person entirely.

She blinked away more tears and spread her hands, hoping he'd understand how profoundly he'd changed her. "You've brought the house alive." She licked her lips and spoke the stark truth. "You've brought me alive."

His smile radiated such warmth, she felt she stepped into summer. "And you've brought me alive."

She was coming to terms with such a marvelous confession, when he went down on one knee and held his hand out toward her. "Margaret Carr, my darling Maggie, will you marry me?"

CHAPTER TWELVE

Joss waited for Maggie to rush into his arms, to say an ecstatic yes, to kiss him. Perhaps even tell him she loved him.

Because he was certain she must.

He wasn't an idiot. Only love made a woman like Maggie Carr give herself to a man. And while she might have kept the words back, her love had illuminated every second of these last incandescent hours.

But to his astonishment, instead of running toward him, she faltered back. An expression that looked like anguish tightened her features, and all the lovely rosy softness vanished in a blink.

"Maggie?" he asked uncertainly, staggering to his feet.

He suddenly felt like a fool. Was he mistaken about her feelings? Had his arrogance alone convinced him that she cared?

The thought that she didn't love him after all crashed down like a landslide, and for a long moment, he couldn't breathe. Joss wasn't a man who prayed much, but faced with her closed expression, he found himself praying that he misunderstood her reaction.

She avoided his eyes and folded her arms across her lovely bosom in an obviously protective gesture. What in Hades did she need to protect herself from? Surely not him. Good God, he was ready to pledge his life to cherishing her.

"Tell me what you're thinking," he said urgently.

The ragged demand made him wince. An hour—ten minutes—ago, he'd have said they were so close, he knew everything in her head and heart.

Now she was a stranger.

Maggie regarded him with the wariness he hadn't seen since he'd arrived. He hated it. He'd believed she trusted him. Hell, she'd come to his bed. What greater statement of trust could she make?

Apart from promising him the rest of her life. And from what he could see, that asked far too much.

"I'm grateful for your offer," she said in a flat voice.

"Grateful?" Baffled rage surged. What the devil was going on? "What blasted sort of namby-pamby response is that to a fellow's proposal?"

She flinched from his tone. "You don't have to do this."

"Have to? What's going on?" He frowned. "I want to marry you, by heaven."

The familiar obstinacy settled on her features. He'd seen it during their first days together, when she'd battled to keep him at a distance.

Well, he'd demolished it before. He could demolish it again. But beneath his bravado lurked desolation.

It was so clear that they belonged together. Why in blazes couldn't she see that, too?

"It's not suitable." She drew herself up, looking as proud as a queen. "I'm a servant."

A servant? God give him strength. He couldn't imagine a woman looking less like a servant.

"Devil take you, of course it's suitable," he snapped.

"Stop shouting at me."

Joss wasn't exactly shouting, but he knew he was acting like a bear instead of a suitor. He struggled to moderate his tone. It was difficult when this meant so damned much—*she* meant so damned much—and she spouted such arrant nonsense.

"I'm sorry." But not as sorry as he was that she hadn't said yes, blast it.

"I don't have to marry you," she said with a hint of truculence.

Joss subjected her to narrow-eyed attention. "No, you don't." Although God help them, if he'd put a baby inside her, she bloody well did. "Forgive me if I mistook your feelings, but I hoped you might *want* to marry me."

She continued to avoid his eyes. That suddenly

struck him as a good sign. The first good sign since his impetuous proposal.

"We've only known each other a couple of days." In a dance of distress, those slender hands twined and untwined at her waist. "We're not far off strangers."

"Piffle," he spat out.

His uncompromising response had her raising surprised eyes to his. He stepped close enough to loom over her. His inconvenient size intimidated most men, but gallant Maggie Carr squared her shoulders and glared. If only she knew how that defiance made her his perfect bride in a way that transcended issues of status or fortune.

His heart crashed against his ribs as he recalled how perfectly they'd fitted together when he'd thrust inside her. She was a fool to deny that they were fated to be together.

Joss went on before she could muster another argument. "If we're strangers, what the hell do you mean by giving yourself to me?"

The delicate jaw set firmer. "You're still shouting."

"No, I'm not." But he paused to run his hand through his hair and suck in an impatient breath. And his voice was marginally quieter when he continued. "Maggie, don't you want to marry me?"

Her lashes fluttered down, and for the first time, he saw the misery beneath her refusal. Hope stirred. Perhaps his case wasn't as lost as he thought.

Curse him for an impulsive idiot. He should have known he'd need more than a romantic setting to convince this superb woman to accept him.

But he'd been so sure of her. Too sure. He wouldn't make that error again.

"It would be wrong."

With a gentleness he should have enlisted from the first, he took her hand. She started without pulling away. Odd that after the many ways he'd touched her tonight, this simple, seemingly innocent contact should seem the most significant.

"Come and sit beside me, sweet Maggie."

She still refused to look at him, although her fingers twined around his with a desperation as revealing as her reluctance to admit she didn't want him. "You'll try to talk me around."

Despite the fraught moment, he couldn't contain a wry smile. "Of course I will."

"And you think I won't be able to resist you."

"I hope," he said, and meant it.

"Just because I slept with you, it doesn't mean you'll always get your way."

He drew her across to a chaise longue and brought her down beside him. "Please make an honest man of me."

"Don't joke," she said in a choked voice.

"I'm not." He paused. "Or only a little. Please marry me, Maggie."

Her hold tightened around his hand. "I can't." Her voice was so low, he had to lean forward to hear her.

"Yes, you can."

At last she turned a stark azure gaze on him. "Then, I won't."

Despair crashed through him at the certainty in her voice. This made no sense. He could have sworn she'd found those moments in his arms as transcendent as he had. "Damn it, my darling, did I do something wrong?"

She frowned. "Of course not."

It wasn't enough. But it was something. "Then why won't you have me?"

Maggie pulled away and stood to face him. He read her pride and her strength. And cursed the possibility that, despite all his advantages, he mightn't prevail.

"You're a man of principle, Joss."

"I'd like to think so." Although he hadn't acted like an honorable man tonight.

"A man of principle doesn't run around, deflowering virgins."

"I did tonight," he said uncomfortably.

"And now you're offering to restore my reputation in the time-honored way."

He must be bloody slow, because it took him a second to understand what she meant. "What the devil?" Genuinely angry, he surged to his feet. "Do you think I'm offering for you, purely for convention's sake?"

As he should have expected, the rage of a six-foot-three brute who must outweigh her twofold didn't send her into retreat. Instead she leveled an unimpressed stare upon him. "Aren't you?"

His hands opened and closed at his sides, as he fought the urge to shake some sense into her. "No, I bloody am not. Didn't you hear what I said? I want to spend the rest of my life with you."

A declaration of love rushed to his lips. But her withering glance killed the words stone dead before he spoke them.

"You're being kind," she said stubbornly.

"I'm not kind," he snarled.

To his surprise, a hint of a smile softened the austere line of her lips. "Of course you are, Joss. You're the kindest person I've ever met."

The compliment didn't please him. Not when she was using it against him.

He spread his hands. "Maggie, don't let your pride consign you to a lonely life." He paused. "And you could be carrying my child. I wasn't as careful as I might have been."

He'd been so drunk on pleasure, he hadn't thought about trying to protect her from pregnancy until it was too late.

In an age-old gesture, her hand crept to cover her belly, and for a fleeting instant, she didn't look like some warrior goddess condemning a mere mortal to eternal banishment. She looked like a young girl facing an uncertain future. "I mightn't be."

"Not good enough." The glance he shot her was a match for any uncompromising attitude she could summon. "I will not have a child of mine born a bastard. You can put aside any noble thoughts of letting me escape the consequences of my acts."

"I'm not being noble," she said, and her voice cracked.

"Neither am I," he said brusquely.

To his horror, tears glittered in her lovely eyes.

"Don't cry, Maggie. For God's sake, don't cry." He reached out, but let his hands drop back to his sides when he saw how distraught she looked. "Would it really be too horrible to marry me? I thought you liked me."

Her lip trembled. "Of course I do."

"Then why?" he asked in bewilderment. "Did I frighten you when we came together? I can be a careless beast, I know. But I promise to do better."

Her tears spilled over and trickled down her pale cheeks. "You didn't frighten me. You're wonderful."

"So wonderful you won't have a bar of me." The air he drew into his lungs tasted as bitter as vinegar. "Instead you want to stay here in this wilderness and forget you ever knew poor lovelorn Josiah Hale."

At last he dared to mention love, but he couldn't blame her for missing it in the rest of what he said.

He'd meant to tell her, once he'd asked her to marry him. But everything had gone wrong after the proposal, and his declaration had shriveled away into silence.

"Oh, Joss," she said on a broken sigh. "You know that's not true."

Sick with wretchedness, he turned away. He'd sworn to make her happy, yet every word he spoke wounded her more deeply. He was a blasted lumbering clodpoll. No wonder she didn't want him.

"I only know the girl I long to marry won't have me."

He stared into the fire and struggled to imagine a future without Maggie at its center. The devil of it was that shouldn't be so difficult. A week ago, he hadn't known she existed. Going on without her shouldn't feel like someone bashed him with a club.

But that was how it did feel. Worse.

Mere hours ago, he'd summoned the will to leave her. But since then, he'd taken her innocence and made a commitment to her in his soul. A commitment that felt stronger than steel.

"If I'm not pregnant, nobody need ever know we came together," she said in a reedy voice.

Joss cleared his throat. Humiliating how one small woman had the power to vanquish him. "I told you I want you. I'm not doing this because I should, but because I can't live without you."

Another bristling silence, before he heard a faltering step behind him. "Is that true?"

He didn't dare turn around, although he sensed she was close behind him. "Of course it's bloody true."

"If it isn't true, I'll never forgive you."

Slowly he turned to face her. She was still crying, which made him want to smash something. "Maggie?"

"Because…" She sucked in a shuddering breath, then spoke in a rush. "Because if you're marrying me out of duty, I couldn't bear it. I love you too much to endure your pity."

He stared into her lovely face and tried to make sense of what he heard. "What did you say?"

She squared her shoulders as she gathered her courage. The stance was familiar. Just so had she greeted him when he'd stumbled into the house—and his destiny—out of a snowstorm. "I said I don't want your pity."

He gave a derisive snort. "As if I'd pity you. You're magnificent."

She frowned in puzzlement. "Thank you," she said, not sounding very sure.

"Anyway, not that bit. The other bit." He stepped within touching distance, and this time he let his hands curl around her slender arms in their loose flannel sleeves. She started at the contact, but didn't move away, thank the Lord. "The bit about loving me."

She had such an expressive face. Joss watched fear

and vulnerability chase each other across her features, before the valor so essential to her nature took over.

"Of course I love you. But that doesn't mean you owe me anything."

It was his turn to frown, even as his heart performed elated cartwheels. She loved him? How could he lose?

"You ask too little of life."

"Life has taught me not to expect much."

"So when happiness comes knocking, you send it away?"

"I said you make me happy."

"For one night, not for a lifetime."

Shock darkened her blue eyes. "I thought you meant to stay with me over Christmas."

"I do," he said seriously. "And past that, for every Christmas the good Lord allows us."

She trembled in his hold. "But only because you think you have to."

"I do have to," he said urgently, and watched despair darken her gaze. "Haven't you been listening? You're the woman I want as my wife. I've never met anyone like you. I've never felt the way I have in the last days. If you make me leave you behind when I ride out of this valley, you're sentencing both of us to a lifetime of heartbreak."

She studied his face as though it was a textbook, and she had a big examination to sit tomorrow. "Joss, I'm not the bride you should choose."

He released one arm and cupped her cheek with the tenderness she always aroused in his heart. "Should has nothing to do with it. You were meant for me, and I was meant for you. Don't make me go on without you."

She kept staring at him, her eyes seeking the answer to some profound question. "Do you mean that?"

Solemnly, he nodded. "With all my soul."

Maggie bit her lip, and he barely resisted the impulse to kiss her. But this fight wasn't about passion, but gaining a commitment from her gallant heart.

"And do you think one day you might love me?" she asked in a small voice.

What a bloody numbskull he was. He'd told Maggie everything, except the most important thing of all. No wonder she still hovered on the brink of saying she'd take him.

Because she was so close to saying yes. He sensed it in the way her body softened and tilted forward. As if the space stretching between them, however narrow, pained her as much as it pained him.

He slid his arms about her. "My darling, don't you know I love you?"

She pushed back against his hold, just as he prepared for her surrender. "No, I don't," she said with a hint of acerbity.

His laugh held a note of exultation. She was a delight, his Maggie.

"You damn well should." His voice deepened into ardor. "I love you. I loved you when I first saw you, although being the blockhead I am, I confused love and lust. It took me far too long to see that I'd found the woman I want for all time, not just for Christmas."

The tension eased from her features, and her eyes lit with what he frantically hoped was happiness. "It didn't take you that long. A few days."

"A few days can change the path of a lifetime. By the time I came back to you tonight, I was in no doubt that I'll love you until the day I die."

Her luscious mouth curved up in a radiant smile. "That's a very nice declaration, Joss."

"I thought my declaration when you first came in was very nice, too."

"It was." She slid her hands up his chest and linked them behind his neck. "But this one was nicer."

Dear God, if he didn't kiss her soon, he'd explode. But he hadn't quite got what he wanted from her. "Nice enough for you to say yes?"

She studied him as if still trying to pierce through to all his secrets. Renewed fear sliced through him, sharp as a knife. Could he fail even now, when they'd both declared their love and surely only a happy ending awaited?

His grip firmed on her waist. "Maggie, please say you'll have me. You'll break both of our hearts if you don't. I swear I'll be a good husband. You'll never regret marrying me. I love you. You love me. We're better together than we ever were apart. Don't condemn me to eternal torment because you've got some bee in your bonnet about being a servant. I don't give a rat's arse about that. Hell, I work for my living. I've got nothing but admiration for how you faced up to your difficult circumstances and made the best of them. That's the girl I want to marry. Someone who will be a true partner. Not some pampered princess who sits around on a cushion all day, waiting to be adored." His voice broke with emotion. "Maggie, please say yes. I'm not a man for romantic words, but you must know how much I need you."

Her stare didn't waver. He had no idea what thoughts lay behind those clear blue eyes.

"Please?" he said unsteadily.

"I think…I think you really do love me," she said in a tone of discovery.

He couldn't resist anymore. He kissed her hard, but broke away before the kiss deepened into passion. "Of course I bloody do. Haven't you been paying attention?"

"Indeed I have." To his surprise, humor lightened her expression. "And you're wrong, you know."

He groaned. "What else must I do to convince you? I'll do anything."

To his surprise, she caressed the back of his neck. "Oh, I'm convinced, Joss."

He was too close to the edge to take her statement for granted. "Then what is it?"

"I can't agree with your claim that you have no gift for words. Nobody could fault this most recent effort."

Joss was so close to despair that he didn't trust what he thought he heard. Although the girl in his hold looked more like the ardent creature who had yielded with such sweetness than she had since his proposal. "But did it work? Will you marry me?"

She rose on her toes and kissed him on the lips with the same ruthless possessiveness he'd shown her. "Oh, yes."

He stared down at her, his disbelief fading into boundless joy. "Soon?"

"Yes."

"And you love me?"

"Yes." As emotion thickened her voice, she trembled in his arms. "More than I ever imagined it was possible to love anyone."

He stared into her eyes and accepted the truth at last. This Christmas brought him a gift more precious than he deserved. He vowed to cherish that gift until the day he died.

"Well, that's good, then," he said, and this time, their kiss was long and passionate and said everything in their hearts.

When he raised his head, Maggie's eyes were so brilliant, he was dazzled. With a ringing laugh, he swung her up into his arms and strode toward the door.

"Joss!" she said, in what he was sure was meant to be a protest, but instead sounded like another declaration of love.

"It's time for all good girls to be in bed, my darling."

"And what about all good boys?"

He kissed her quickly and lowered his voice to a growl. "Oh, my love, once I get you back into bed, I intend to be very good indeed."

EPILOGUE

Thorncroft Hall, Yorkshire, 24th December 1826

Maggie Hale loved Christmas Eve almost as much as she loved Christmas Day, which in recent years had become a rambunctious, laughter-filled celebration of family love.

She paused at the top of the carved oak staircase and surveyed the bustling hall below, decorated with greenery and candles, and hung with mistletoe brought from the Hale family home in Sussex. In one corner, Joss's brothers and sisters crowded around the piano singing carols. In another, the more senior members of the party, including Dr. Black, sat beside the fire, sharing reminiscences of Christmases past. In the center of the room, the older children, nieces and nephews and cousins, played snapdragon and other Christmas games. Their excited laughter rose to the rafters. The youngest children had been sent to bed an hour ago.

Joss's tall, handsome father, an older, more grizzled version of Maggie's husband, had joined the snapdragon game with a gusto that put his grandchildren to shame. She watched her old friend Jane come in, bearing a tray of cakes. Jane remained at Thorncroft Hall, but these days, her daughter and son-in-law augmented the household staff. With the addition of Jane's four grandchildren as well, Thorncroft was no longer the lonely, echoing barn of a place it had been when only Jane and Maggie rattled around inside it.

The Thorncroft estate had changed, too, now containing a complex of elegant buildings. Instead of ordering changes to the manor, Dr. Black had built three new lodges to Joss's design, out of sight of the main house. Perfect for an influx of guests like this.

This year, the Festive Season was special for so many reasons. Not least because this was the first Christmas that she and Joss spent where their love had begun.

They played host to their family and friends. During the past six months, Dr. Black had transferred ownership of the estate to Joss. Maggie became the chatelaine where for so many years, she'd been a servant.

The fact still had the power to astonish her.

Joss came up behind her and slid his arms around her waist. She'd known he was there before he touched her. They'd reached such a level of closeness that she could sense his presence from a couple of rooms away.

"Our daughter is a demanding chit," he said, drawing Maggie back against him. She basked in the warmth of his big body, familiar and beloved.

"Arabella wouldn't let you go without reading her a second story?"

Their four-year-old girl was clever and pretty and imperious, and knew she had her papa twined around her little finger. Maggie remembered the wonder in Joss's expression the first time he saw his newborn daughter. He'd been the little girl's slave ever since.

"I'm lucky I escaped before midnight. And that might have put our private celebrations back an hour or two, my love."

Anticipation heated her blood. She and Joss always marked the night they'd come together as their true anniversary, instead of Valentine's Day when they'd married at his parish church in Sussex. Oh, how Maggie still thrilled to recall those winter nights of sensual discovery five years ago, when they'd had this rambling manor house all to themselves.

It had taken some contriving to place a gloss of propriety on a courtship begun so unconventionally. Joss had left her on Twelfth Night, the day before Jane returned from Goathland as the proud grandmother of a baby girl.

He'd arrived, ostensibly as a stranger, to meet and fall in love with Maggie at first sight. Not, as he said, that far from the truth.

Within a couple of weeks, he'd invited his parents to Fraedale to meet his betrothed. Maggie and Joss had then traveled south in a family party for a February ceremony, all chaperoned and above board.

How difficult it had been to sleep alone during those nights before the wedding, when Maggie had to pretend she was an appropriately virginal fiancée. Luckily, Arabella had arrived a respectable nine months after their nuptials, almost to the day.

Maggie glanced up at her husband. "Your son and heir couldn't wait for me to go back to the party, so he could sneak out of bed to play with his blocks by the light of the moon."

Thomas, three years old, and much quieter than his sister, was fascinated with building and the way things worked. Her husband's brilliance as a designer had clearly descended upon the next generation.

Joss's embrace tightened, and he kissed the top of her head. "We've been lucky, haven't we?"

Maggie still delighted in his casual gestures of affection. After her lonely years, she'd never take Joss's love for granted.

As she snuggled closer, a secret smile curved her lips. "Yes, we have."

She raised a hand to press his palm to her midriff, just above where their next baby grew. Tonight she'd tell him the news in the privacy of their room, the room where they'd first shared a bed.

"It's good to be back. You know, we could live here six months of the year and six months in London."

"I'd love that," Maggie said. "But can you leave your practice so long?"

"I can bring work up with me. In summer, getting in and out of Fraedale isn't so difficult."

"It is in winter."

His soft chuckle brushed across her skin like velvet. "Winter here has other compensations."

"Yes," she said on a reminiscent sigh.

Below them, Joss's mother Kitty was clearing a space for dancing. Maggie loved Kitty, who had welcomed her from the first and never shown any sign of minding that her handsome, successful son had chosen a girl who worked as a servant.

"And the practice has people lining up with commissions." Joss's architectural business was thriving. Another secret they kept this Christmas was the knighthood that became official in the New Year. Maggie Carr, humble housekeeper, would step into 1827 as Margaret, Lady Hale. The change still struck her as hard to credit. "I can afford to play the lord of the manor now and again."

"Especially when you are the lord of the manor. How generous Dr. Black was to give us this estate."

"Absurdly so. I'm so glad Uncle Thomas is here this Christmas."

"He and his namesake have established quite the alliance. I suspect he might end up visiting Thorncroft more often, now he's given it away, than he did when he owned it." She stroked Joss's large, capable hand. "The house has come alive. It's hard to recall what it was like before you burst into my life."

"You were so stern when I turned up on your doorstep."

A huff of wry amusement escaped her. "Your fatal charm soon proved my downfall."

"Will my fatal charm lure you away now, to start our special Christmas Eve?"

"Tempting." She caught Kitty's eye, as her mother-in-law glanced up from the crowded hall. "We have guests."

"Who are all staying until after New Year."

"Perhaps we can slip out in an hour."

"I sometimes think you married me purely to become part of my family," he said with mock self-pity.

She smiled, in a mood to tease. "I'm so sorry you've finally realized the sad truth."

"They love you nearly as much as I do." He presented his arm. "Shall we go downstairs, my lovely wife?"

Once down in the hubbub, there were no more chances for quiet conversation. Instead Joss was caught up in a riotous game of blind man's bluff that tripped up more than one dancer, while Maggie joined the older folk around the fire.

It was well beyond the promised hour when Maggie at last found herself dancing a waltz in her husband's arms.

"Shall we retire soon? Nobody will miss us." Joss smiled down at her. "Although it seems unkind to remove the prettiest girl from the party."

Dizzy with love and happiness—it was hard to keep a sensible tongue in her head when all her dreams had come true so magnificently—she smiled back at the man she adored. "You're too kind, sir."

"No, I'm not, by God." He whirled her around, until they came to a breathless halt beneath an elaborate arrangement of mistletoe and red and gold ribbon suspended from the beams. "You're still the most beautiful girl I've ever seen."

His kiss was more circumspect than usual—after all, they had an audience—but it still told her how deeply he loved her.

"Oh, Joss, I do love you," she whispered as he drew away. And blushed when she saw that Kitty and Dr. Black had stopped close enough to overhear her fervent declaration.

Dr. Black viewed them with an unaccustomed misty expression in his faded gray eyes behind their round spectacles. In the last five years, she'd seen more of him than she had in all the time she'd worked at Thorncroft. She'd become very fond of him, although she'd never quite overcome her awareness that once he'd paid her wages.

"Kitty, I'm so glad you wrote to me all those years ago and suggested I find Joss a wife. Putting my godson and Margaret together was a stroke of genius."

"Thomas, you know that was a secret between us," Kitty said in horror, as a fraught silence crashed down around them.

Maggie frowned at her former employer. "But you didn't put us together."

"Yes, I did." Dr. Black, who had been enjoying the Christmas punch, blinked at her owlishly. "Wrote to Joss saying I wanted the place modernized, so he'd come up to stay. When any nitwit can see Thorncroft is perfect as it is. Then wrote to you to say to expect him."

Joss's arms had dropped from her waist, and some quality in his stance made her shoot him a curious glance. "Joss?" she asked. "What's wrong?"

He was frowning into the distance. She stared at him baffled, before she recalled a conversation from their early days as man and wife. He'd smugly declared that he'd found his own bride, and just the right bride for him, without benefit of his mamma's enthusiastic matchmaking.

Oh, no. Did he imagine Maggie had set out to trap him with the conniving of his marriage-minded mother? Surely he must know his wife had never deceived him. Surely he must remember how unprepared she'd been for his arrival, that night of the snowstorm.

She narrowed her eyes at him. "Whatever it is

you're thinking, stop it right now." She turned to Dr. Black. "I'm sorry, sir. I received no such letter."

Dr. Black, seemingly unaware of the strained atmosphere, beamed at them both. "Maybe I didn't get around to writing to you, Margaret. I know I wrote to the boy. Not sure I wrote to Kitty either, now I come to think of it. But I definitely leaped to answer her plea to find my godson a suitable bride."

"And you did that, Thomas," Kitty said, casting her son a doubtful look. His reticence was becoming noticeable. "But it was purely good fortune that Joss and Maggie fell in love."

"So our meeting wasn't a lucky accident after all," Maggie said, trying to sound lighthearted.

No wonder Joss's family had expressed no surprise when he found his future wife in an out of the way corner of Yorkshire and brought her home for a quick wedding. They must have already been bracing for her arrival.

"It was a lucky accident," Kitty said with a hint of desperation, when Joss still didn't speak.

"With a lot of help from me," Dr. Black said, earning him another glare from Kitty.

"You're a very unlikely cupid, Thomas," Kitty said acidly.

Maggie was still staring at Joss, not understanding his odd reaction. "Do you mind so much, Joss?"

Joss blinked, and Maggie watched the life and

warmth flow back into his face. The green eyes he focused on her were once more radiant with love.

"You know," he said in a thoughtful voice, "once upon a time, I might have. But now I really don't."

"I know you hate to feel manipulated," she said steadily. "But I wasn't part of any plot."

"I wasn't plotting," Kitty said, offended.

"Yes, you were," Joss said, although affection deprived the words of rancor.

"Perhaps a little," Kitty sheepishly admitted.

Dr. Black at last picked up the less than positive response to his self-congratulations. "Have I put my foot in it?"

Joss reached out to catch Maggie's hand and brought it to his lips. "Forgive my distraction, my darling. I had to rearrange my memories of our courtship, so they fit the new picture."

Maggie regarded him with a frown, not wanting this nonsense to spoil what had been such a lovely day. "You mightn't have liked me when you met me. It's not as if you had no choice in what happened."

He squeezed her hand. "Of course I had no choice."

"Josiah Hale!" his mother protested, even as he continued.

"Maggie, you are the woman I was fated to love. From the moment I first saw you, I couldn't resist you." Leaving her gratified—and relieved—after his ardent declaration, he turned to Dr. Black. "Uncle Thomas, thank you from the bottom of my heart. If you're the author of my present happiness, I owe you more than I can ever repay."

Dr. Black's cheerful humor revived, and he bestowed another glowing smile on Maggie and Joss. A smile perhaps a few degrees brighter, thanks to the brandy enlivening the punch.

"Knew it was the perfect solution." He turned back to Kitty. "Let me know if you want my help with any other unmarried sprigs littering your life, my dear Kitty. I'll find them all a pretty girl to wed, just like Maggie. Although they'll have to be pretty indeed to hold a candle to you in your heyday, by George."

"Time for us to go, my love," Joss said in an undertone. As he tugged Maggie away toward the staircase, she watched her self-possessed mother-in-law blush and kiss Dr. Black's cheek.

"Joss, you're not really angry with Dr. Black for setting up our meeting, are you?"

"Angry?" Joss's relaxed laugh soothed her last niggling worry. "If I hadn't already named my son after him, I'd be ready to do it again. We can christen all our future children Thomas. Even the girls."

She gave a choked gulp of amusement and leaned in, close enough to murmur for his ears alone, "Let's come up with something different for the new baby. It would be so inconvenient to call for one child and get the whole lot turning up to answer."

Joss stopped so abruptly at the base of the stairs, she stumbled into him. "The new baby?"

She smiled to see the wonder illuminating his expression. "Next summer, I think."

"Oh, my glorious beloved, I couldn't adore you more." He seized her up for a passionate kiss that this time paid no heed to observers.

And Maggie kissed her husband back with every ounce of love in her overflowing heart.

THE WINTER WIFE

CHAPTER ONE

North Yorkshire, Christmas Eve, 1825

The crash of shattering wood and the terrified screams of horses pierced the frosty night like a knife.

Sebastian Sinclair, Earl of Kinvarra, swore, brought his restive mount under control, then spurred the animal around the turn in the snowy road. With icy clarity, the full moon lit the white landscape, starkly revealing the disaster before him.

A flashy black curricle lay on its side in a ditch, the hood up against the weather. One horse had broken free and now wandered the roadway, harness dragging. The other plunged wildly in the traces, struggling to escape.

Swiftly Kinvarra dismounted, knowing his mare would await his signal, and ran to free the distressed horse. As he slid down the muddy ditch, a hatless man scrambled out of the smashed curricle.

"Are you hurt?" Kinvarra asked, casting a quick eye over him.

"No, I thank you, sir." The effete blond fellow turned back to the carriage. "Come, darling. Let me assist you."

A graceful black-gloved hand extended from inside, and a cloaked woman emerged with more aplomb than Kinvarra would have believed possible in the circumstances. Indications were that neither traveler was injured, so he concentrated on the trapped horse. When he spoke soothingly to the terrified beast, it quieted to panting stillness, exhausted with thrashing. While Kinvarra checked its legs, murmuring calm assurances, the stranger helped the lady up to the roadside.

The horse shook itself and with a few ungainly jumps, ascended the bank to trot along the road toward its partner. Neither animal seemed to suffer worse than fright, a miracle considering that the curricle was beyond repair.

"Madam, are you injured?" Kinvarra asked as he climbed the ditch. He stuck his riding crop under his arm and brushed his gloved hands together to knock the clinging snow from them.

It was a hellishly cold night. Christmas tomorrow

would be a chilly affair. But then of course his Christmases had been chilly for years, no matter the weather.

The woman kept her head down. With shock? With shyness? For the sake of propriety? Perhaps he'd stumbled on some elopement or clandestine meeting.

"Madam?" he asked again, more sharply. Whatever her fear of scandal, he needed to know if she required medical assistance.

"Sweeting?" The yellow-haired fop bent to peer into the shadows cast by her hood. "Are you sure you're unharmed? Speak, my dove. Your silence troubles my soul."

While Kinvarra digested the man's outlandish phrasing, the woman stiffened and drew away. "For heaven's sake, Harold, you're not giving a recitation at a musicale." With an impatient gesture, she flung back her hood and glared straight at Kinvarra.

Even though he'd identified her the moment she spoke, he found himself staring dumbstruck into her face. A piquant, vivid, pointed face under an untidy tumble of luxuriant gold hair.

Furious and incredulous, he wheeled on the milksop. "What the devil are you doing with my wife?"

Alicia Sinclair, Countess of Kinvarra, was bruised, angry, uncomfortable, and agonizingly embarrassed. Not to mention suffering the aftereffects of her choking terror when the toppling carriage had tossed her around like a pebble in a torrent.

Even so, her heart lurched into the wayward dance it always performed at the merest sight of Sebastian.

She'd been married for eleven miserable years. Their short interval living as man and wife had been wretched. She disliked her husband more than any other man in the world. But nothing prevented her gaze from clinging to every line of that narrow, intense face with its high cheekbones, long, arrogant nose and sharply angled jaw. He looked older than the last time she'd seen him, more cynical if that was possible. But still handsome, still compelling, still vital in a way nobody else she knew could match.

Damn him to Hades, he remained the most magnificent creature she'd ever beheld.

Such a pity his soul was as black as his glittering eyes.

"After all this time, I'm flattered you recognize me, my lord," she said silkily.

"Lord Kinvarra, this is a surprise," Harold stammered, faltering back as if anticipating violence. "You must wonder why I accompany the lady—"

Oh, Harold, act the man, even if the hero is beyond your reach. You're safe. Kinvarra doesn't care enough about me to kill you.

Although even the most indifferent husband took it ill when his wife chose a lover. And Kinvarra had always suffered an overabundance of pride. There wasn't the slightest hope that he'd mistake Alicia's reasons for traveling on this isolated road in the middle of the night. She stifled a rogue pang of guilt.

Curse Kinvarra, she had absolutely nothing to feel guilty about.

"I've recalled your existence every quarter these past ten years, my love," her husband said equally smoothly, ignoring Harold's dismayed interjection. Although the faint trace of Scottish brogue in Kinvarra's deep voice indicated that he reined in his temper. His breath formed white clouds on the frigid air. "I'm perforce reminded when I pay your allowance. A substantial investment upon which I receive woefully little return."

"It warms the cockles of my heart to know that I linger in your thoughts," she sniped.

She refused to cower like a wet hen before his banked anger. He sounded reasonable, calm, controlled, but she had no trouble reading the tension in his broad shoulders or in the way his powerful hands opened and closed at his sides as if he'd dearly like to hit something.

"In faith, my lady, you speak false. Creatures of ice have no use for a heart." A faint, malicious smile lifted the corners of his mouth. "Should I warn this paltry fellow that he risks frostbite in your company?"

She steeled herself against Kinvarra's taunting. He couldn't hurt her now. He hadn't been able to hurt her since she'd left him. Any twinge was merely the result of temporary shakiness after the accident. That was all. It couldn't be because this man retained the power to stick needles into her feelings.

"My lord, egad, I protest." Fortunately, shock made Harold sound less like a frightened sheep. "The lady is your wife. Surely she merits your chivalry at the very least."

Harold had never seen her in her husband's company, and some reluctant and completely misplaced loyalty to Kinvarra meant she hadn't explained why the Sinclairs lived apart. The accepted fiction was that the earl and his countess were polite strangers who by mutual design rarely met.

Poor Harold, he was about to discover the nasty truth that the earl and his countess loathed each other.

"Like hell she does," Kinvarra muttered, casting her an incendiary glance under long dark eyelashes.

Alicia was human enough to wish the bright moonlight didn't reveal quite so much of her husband's seething rage. But the fate that proved capricious enough to fling them together tonight of all nights wasn't likely to heed her pleas.

"Do you intend to present your cicisbeo?" Kinvarra's voice remained quiet. She'd long ago learned that was when he was most lethal.

Dear God, did he plan to shoot Harold after all?

Her hands clenched in her skirts as fear tightened her throat. Lacerating as Kinvarra's tongue could be, he'd never shown her a moment's violence. But did that extend to the man she planned to take into her bed? Kinvarra was a crack shot and a famous swordsman. If it came to a duel, Harold wouldn't stand a chance.

"My lord, I protest the description," Harold bleated, sidling further away. He'd clearly also heard the unspoken threat in Kinvarra's question.

Oh, for pity's sake. Was it too much to wish that her suitor would stand up to the scoundrel she'd married as a silly chit of seventeen?

Alicia drew a deep breath of freezing air and reminded herself that she favored Lord Harold Fenton precisely because he wasn't an overbearing brute like her husband. Harold was a scholar and a poet, a man of the mind. She should consider it a mark of Harold's superior intelligence that he was wary of Kinvarra.

But her insistence didn't convince her traitorous heart.

How she wished she really was the callous witch Kinvarra called her. Then she'd be immune both to his insults and to this insidious attraction that she'd never conquered, no matter how she tried.

"My lady?" Kinvarra asked, still in that even voice that struck a chill into her soul sharper than the winter wind. "Who is this…gentleman?"

She stiffened her backbone and leveled her shoulders. She was made of stronger stuff than this. Never would she let her husband guess that he still had power over her.

Her response was steady. "Lord Kinvarra, allow me to present Lord Harold Fenton."

Harold performed an uncertain bow without stepping any nearer. "My lord."

As he straightened, tense silence descended. Alicia shifted to try and warm up her icy feet, fulminating against the bad luck that threw her in Kinvarra's way.

"Well, this is awkward," Kinvarra said flatly, although she saw in his taut, dark face that his anger hadn't abated one whit.

"I don't see why," Alicia snapped.

It wasn't just her husband who tried her patience. There was her lily-livered lover and the perishing cold. The temperature must have dropped ten degrees in the last five minutes. She shivered, then silently cursed that Kinvarra noticed and Harold didn't. Harold was too busy staring at her husband the way a mouse stared at an adder.

"Do you imagine I'm so sophisticated that I'll ignore discovering you in the arms of another man? My dear, you do me too much credit."

She stifled the urge to consign Kinvarra to perdition. Just as she stifled the poignant memory that once he'd called her his dear and his love and he'd meant it. Once, briefly, long ago.

"If you'll set aside your bruised vanity for the moment, you'll understand that we merely require you to ride to the nearest habitation and request help. Then you and I can return to acting like mere acquaintances, my lord."

He laughed, and she struggled to suppress the sensual awareness that rippled down her spine at the soft, deep sound. "Some things haven't changed, I see. You're still dishing out orders. And I'm still damned if I'll play your lapdog."

"Can you see another solution?" she asked sweetly.

"Yes," he said with a snap of his straight white teeth. "I can leave you to freeze. Not that you'd notice. Your blood has always been colder than Satan's icehouse."

Her pride insisted that she send him on his way with a flea in his ear. The weather—and what common sense remained under the urge to wound that always flared in Kinvarra's vicinity—prompted her to sound more conciliatory.

It was late. She and Harold hadn't passed anyone on this country road. Bleak, snowy moors extended for miles around them. The grim truth was that if Kinvarra didn't help, they were stranded until morning. And while she was dressed in good thick wool, she wasn't prepared for enduring a night in the open. The chill of the ground seeped through her fur-lined boots, and she shifted again, trying to revive feeling in her frozen feet.

"My lord..." During the year they'd lived together, she'd called him Sebastian. During their few meetings since, she'd clung to formality to keep him at a distance. "My lord, there's no point in quarreling. Basic charity compels your assistance. I would consider myself in your debt if you fetch aid as quickly as possible."

He arched one black eyebrow in an imperious fashion that made her want to clout him. Not a new sensation. "Now that's something I'd like to see."

"What?"

"Gratitude."

He knew he had her at a disadvantage, and he wasn't likely to rise above that fact. She ground her teeth and battled to retain her manners. "It's all I can offer."

The smile that curved his lips was pure devilry. A shiver with no connection to the cold ran through her.

"Your imagination fails you, my dear countess."

Her throat closed with nerves—and that reluctant physical reaction she couldn't ignore. He hadn't shifted, yet suddenly she felt threatened. Which was ludicrous. During all their years apart, he'd given no indication he wanted anything from her except her absence. One chance meeting wasn't likely to turn him into a robber baron, ready to spirit her away to his lonely tower where he could have his way with her.

Having his way with her was the last thing Kinvarra wanted, as she was humiliatingly aware.

Nonetheless, she had to fight the urge to retreat. She knew from dispiriting experience that her only chance of handling Kinvarra was to feign control. "What do you want?"

This time he did lean closer, until his great height

overshadowed her. Close enough for her to think that if she stretched out one hand, she'd touch that powerful chest, those wide shoulders. "I want—"

There was a piercing whinny and a sudden pounding of hooves on the snow. Appalled, disbelieving, Alicia turned to see Harold galloping off on one of the carriage horses, legs flailing as he struggled for purchase without stirrups.

"Harold?"

Her voice faded to nothing in the night. Her beau didn't slow down. In fact, he kicked his mount's sides to encourage greater speed. She'd been so engrossed in her battle with Kinvarra, she hadn't even noticed that Harold had caught one of the stray horses.

Kinvarra's low laugh mocked her. "Oh, my dear. Commiserations. Your swain proves a sad disappointment. I wonder if he's fleeing my temper or yours. You really have no luck in love, have you?"

She was too astonished to be upset at Harold's departure. Instead she focused on Kinvarra. Her voice turned hard. "No luck in husbands, at any rate."

Kinvarra suffered Alicia's hate-filled regard and wondered what the hell he was going to do with his troublesome wife out in this frigid wilderness. The insolent baggage deserved to be left where she stood, but even he, who owed her repayment for countless slights over the years, wouldn't do that to her.

It seemed he had no choice but to help.

Not that she'd thank him. He had no illusions that after she'd got what she wanted—a warm bed, a roof over her head and a decent meal—she'd forget any promises of gratitude.

In spite of the punishing cold, heat flooded him as he briefly let himself imagine Alicia's gratitude. She'd shed that heavy red cloak. She'd let down that mass of gold hair until it tumbled around her shoulders. Then she'd kiss him as if she didn't hate him, and she'd—

From long habit, he stopped before the flaring images became too interesting. A thousand fantasies had sustained him the first year of their separation, but he'd learned for sanity's sake to control them since. Now they only troubled him after his rare meetings with his wife.

This was the longest time he and Alicia had spent together in years. It should remind him why he eschewed her company. Instead, it reminded him that she was the only woman who had ever challenged him, the only woman who had ever matched him in strength, the only woman he couldn't forget, desperately as he'd tried.

He smiled into her sulky, beautiful face. "Poor Alicia. It seems you're stuck with me."

How that must smart. The long ride to his Yorkshire manor on this desolate night suddenly offered a myriad of pleasures, not least of which was the chance to knock a few chips off his wife's monumental pride.

She didn't respond to his comment. Instead with an unreadable expression, she stared after her absconding lover. "We're only about five miles from Harold's hunting lodge."

The wench didn't even try to lie about the assignation, blast her impudence. "If he manages to stay on that horse, Horace should make it."

Fenton showed no great skill as a bareback rider. Even as Kinvarra recognized the wish as unworthy, he hoped the blackguard ended up on his rump in a muddy hedgerow.

"Harold," she said absently, drawing her cloak tight around her slender throat. "You could take me there."

This time his laughter was unconstrained. She'd always had nerve, his wife, even when she'd been little more than an untried girl.

"Be damned if you think I'm carting you off to cuckold me in comfort, madam."

She sent him a cool look. "I'm thinking purely in terms of shelter, my lord."

"I'm sure," he said cynically.

Still, whatever his jaded view of the world and its inhabitants, he couldn't completely stifle his rankling surprise that Alicia had at last chosen a lover. In spite of their lack of communication, he'd always known what she was up to.

Since leaving him, she'd been remarkably chaste,

which was one of the reasons he'd allowed the ridiculous separation to continue. Clearly living with him for a year had left her with no taste for bed sport. A bitter acknowledgement for a man to make, by God.

Recent gossip had mentioned Lord Harold Fenton as a persistent suitor, but Kinvarra thought he knew enough of his wife to consider the second son of the Marquess of Granville poor competition. Bugger it, he should have listened to the gossip.

By all that was holy, her taste had deteriorated since she'd abandoned her marriage. The man was a complete nonentity.

Perhaps one day she'd thank her husband for saving her from a disastrous mistake.

And the bleak and stony moor around them might suddenly sprout coconut palms.

"No, my love, your fate is sealed." He slapped his riding crop against his boot and tilted his hat more securely on his head with an arrogant gesture designed to irritate her. "Horatio travels north. I travel south. Unless you intend to ride the other carriage horse or pursue the clodpoll on foot, your direction is mine."

"Does that mean you will help me?" This time, she didn't bother correcting his deliberate misremembering of her suitor's name.

She was lucky he didn't call the toad Habakkuk and skewer his kidneys with a rapier. Alicia was his. Kinvarra had known that from the first moment he saw her, slender, unsure, but full of a wild vitality that still beckoned to him, whatever else divided them. No other damned rapscallion was going to steal her away. Especially a rapscallion who lacked the spine to fight for her.

Kinvarra strode across to his bay mare and snatched up the reins. "If you ask nicely."

To his surprise, Alicia laughed. "Devil take you, Kinvarra."

He swung into the saddle and urged the horse nearer to his wife. "Indubitably, my dear."

Her suddenly cavalier attitude made it easier to deal with her, but it puzzled him. Her lover's desertion hadn't cast her down.

If she didn't care for the fellow, why in Hades accept his advances? Yet again, Kinvarra realized how far he remained from understanding the complicated creature he'd wed with such high hopes eleven years ago.

He extended one leather-gloved hand and noted her hesitation before she accepted his assistance. It was the first time he'd touched her since she'd left him, and even through two layers of leather, he felt the burning shock of contact. She stiffened, as though she too felt that unwelcome surge of response.

He'd always wanted her. That was part of the problem, God help them. He'd often asked himself if time would erode the attraction.

Just one touch of her hand on this snowy night, and he received his unequivocal answer.

She swung onto the horse behind him and paused again before looping her arms around his waist. He'd always been hellish aware of her reactions, and he couldn't help but note her reluctance to touch him.

Good God, what was wrong with the woman? She'd been ready enough to do more than touch rabbit-hearted Fenton. Surely her long-suffering husband deserved a little friendliness after coming to her rescue. With damned little encouragement, too, he might add.

Compared to the cold night, she felt warm and soft against his back. His lunatic heart dipped at her nearness, even as he told himself that the warmth and softness were lies. Alicia Sinclair was made of stone. Or at least she was when it came to her husband. If he forgot that, she'd drag his soul through the razor-sharp thorns of hell again.

But the warning fell on deaf ears. When she touched him, he could think of little else but how long it was since he'd held her in his arms and shown her how strongly she inflamed his unruly passions.

The mare curveted under the double weight, but Kinvarra settled her with a curt word. He never had trouble with horses. It was his wife he couldn't control.

"What about my belongings?" she asked, calm as you please.

The lady should demonstrate proper shame at being caught with a lover. But of course, that wasn't Alicia. She held her head high, whatever destiny threw at her.

It was one of the things he loved about her.

He quashed the unwelcome insight. "There's an inn a few miles ahead. I'll get them to send someone for your baggage."

He clicked his tongue to the horse and cantered in the opposite direction to the one Fenton had taken. Which was lucky for the weasel. If Kinvarra caught up with Fenton now, he'd be inclined to reach for his horsewhip. What right had that bastard to interfere with other men's wives, then scuttle away leaving the lady stranded?

Alicia settled herself more comfortably, pressing her lovely, lush body into his back. She hadn't been this close to him in years. He was scoundrel enough to enjoy the contact, however reluctantly she granted it.

Maybe after all, he should be grateful to old Harold. He might even send the poltroon a case of port and a note of appreciation.

Well, that might go too far.

"Is that where we're heading?" She tightened her arms. He wished it was because she wanted to touch him and not just because she sought a more secure seat. He also wished that when she said "we", his belly didn't cramp with longing for the word to be true.

Damn Alicia. She'd always held magic for him, and she always would. Ten long years without her had taught him that grim lesson.

The reminder of the dance she'd led him made him

respond in a clipped tone. "No, we're going to Heseltine Hall near Whitby."

"But you can leave me at the inn, can't you?"

"It's a poor place. I couldn't abandon a woman there without protection."

He tried, he really did, to keep the satisfaction from his voice, but he must have failed. He felt her tense against his back, although she couldn't pull too far away without risking a fall.

"And who's going to protect me from you?" she muttered, almost as if to herself.

"I mean you no harm." For all their difficult interactions, he'd only ever wished her well. "You didn't come all the way from London in that spindly carriage, did you?"

"It's inappropriate to discuss my arrangement with Lord Harold," she said coldly.

He laughed again, against all sense, enchanted with her spirit. "Humor me."

She sighed. "We traveled up separately to York." Her voice melted into sincerity, and he tried not to respond to the husky sweetness. "I truly didn't set out to cause a scandal. You and I parted in rancor, but I have no ambition to damage you or your name."

"Whatever your attempts at discretion, you still meant to give yourself to that puppy," Kinvarra bit out, all amusement abruptly fled.

Alicia didn't answer.

CHAPTER TWO

The weather had worsened by the time they reached the inn. Alicia realized as they approached the ramshackle, rambling building that it was indeed the rough place Kinvarra had described. But just the prospect of shelter and a chance to rest her aching body was welcome. Surely Kinvarra couldn't intend to ride on to his mysterious manor tonight when more snow fell every minute and their horse was blowing with exhaustion.

The earl dismounted and lifted her from the saddle. His hands were firm around her waist, and she struggled to ignore the thrill that sizzled through her traitorous body. The lamps that lit the inn yard revealed that he looked tired and strangely, for a man who always seemed so indomitable, unhappy.

As he set her upon the cobblestones, his hands didn't linger. She tried not to note that she'd touched

Kinvarra more in the last few hours than she had since she'd left him. Nor did she wish to remember that hugging his strong back, she'd felt safer than she had in years.

"Let's get you into the warmth." He gestured for her to precede him inside, as a groom rushed to take their horse.

Alicia had expected her husband to spend the journey haranguing her for her wantonness—or at the very least her idiocy in setting out for the wilds of Yorkshire in the depths of winter so ill prepared for disaster. But he'd remained quiet.

How she wished he'd berated her. She dearly needed to remember why she hated him. She'd spent a decade convincing herself that leaving him had been her only choice of action. A moment's unexpected kindness shouldn't change that.

While his body offered a warm anchor and his adept hands unerringly guided their horse toward sanctuary, resentment had proven fiendishly difficult to maintain. When she wasn't constantly sniping at him, it became impossible to ignore his physical presence. His clean, male scent—horses, leather, soap, fresh air. The muscles under her hands, hard even through his winter clothing. His lean strength.

Kinvarra had been a handsome boy. He'd become a splendid man.

She'd forgotten how powerfully he affected her. And the pity of it was that she'd need far too long after this to forget again. He made every other man pale into insignificance.

It was vilely irritating.

The rotund landlord greeted them at the door, clearly overwhelmed to have the quality on his humble premises. The tap room was jammed to the rafters with people bundled up for an uncomfortable night on chairs and benches. A few hardy souls hunched near the fire, drinking and smoking. One table of revelers even defied their circumstances and sang some carols in honor of the season.

Apart from a couple of serving maids, Alicia was the only woman present. Self-consciously she drew her hood around her face, as she shifted closer to the blaze. The heat penetrated frozen extremities with painful force. Even molding herself to Kinvarra's big, strong body, the ride had been frozen purgatory.

For all that she remained standing, she'd drifted into a half-doze when she became aware of Kinvarra beside her. He spoke in a low voice to save them from eavesdroppers. "My lady, there's a difficulty."

Blinking, striving to regain alertness, she slowly turned to face him. "I'm happy to accept any accommodation. Surely you don't plan to go on tonight."

He shook his head. He'd taken off his hat, and light sheened across his thick dark hair. "The weather will worsen before it improves. It would be cruel to force my horse back into the blizzard. And there isn't another village for miles."

"Then of course we'll stay."

His saturnine face was shuttered. "Are you sure?"

His hesitancy aroused misgivings. Her husband was never hesitant. "What is it?"

"There's only one room."

One room? Dear heaven. What a catastrophe. Aghast, she stared at him. "Surely...surely you could sleep in the tap room."

The moment she made the suggestion, she felt like the world's most ungrateful creature. Her husband had rescued her in extremely good spirit, given the compromising situation he caught her in. He'd made a few cutting remarks, but she'd deserved much worse. Like her, he was tired and cold and hungry. It wasn't fair to consign him to a hard floor and the company of a parcel of rustics, not to mention the vermin flourishing on their unwashed persons.

His lips twisted in a wry smile. "As you can see, there's no space. Even if there was, I won't leave you on your own with the place full of God knows what ruffians."

What on earth was going on here? He sounded protective. When she knew he despised everything about her. "We can't share a room."

She'd suspect him of some trick, if she wasn't sharply aware that he, too, recalled the misery of their time together at Balmuir House. He must be as eager as she for this night to end so they could both return to their separate lives. Kinvarra would never plot the seduction of his wife.

So what was his game?

His eyes glinted with sardonic amusement. "I don't see why not. We're married. It's too late to play Miss Propriety. After all, you were about to hop into bed with Herbert."

"Harold," she said automatically, avoiding his gaze.

Sick humiliation twisted her belly into knots. Here with Kinvarra, she didn't feel brave and daring for taking a lover. Instead she felt grubby and small.

His features tightened into harshness. "Whatever the bugger's name, I hope to hell he hasn't sampled your favors already, or I'll think even less of his stalwart behavior on the road."

"We hadn't...we didn't..." She stopped and glowered at him, furious. "That is none of your concern, my lord."

But it was far too late. Triumph lit Kinvarra's face. Curse her for confessing that she was still to all intents faithful to him. The cad didn't deserve her fidelity. He never had.

"Can't we hire a gig to take us to your manor?" she asked on a note of desperation.

Now the prospect of staying at the inn wasn't so welcome. And not just because she'd have to share a room with her husband. Tonight's events left her too exposed to painful memories and present confusion. Easy to play the indifferent spouse when she met the earl for five minutes in a crowded ballroom. Much more difficult when she'd just spent an hour cuddled up to him, and he sounded like a reasonable man, instead of the spoiled, petulant boy she recalled from their brief cohabitation.

At least, thank heaven, he wouldn't touch her, whatever silly suspicions entered her mind. She was safe from that. The last time they exchanged more than bland public greetings, he'd made it obvious that he'd rather have a crocodile in his bed.

He shook his head. "There are none. And even if there were, I'm not going to risk my neck—and yours —on a night like this. Face it, madam, you've returned to the bonds of holy matrimony until tomorrow. I wager you'll survive the experience."

Alicia wasn't so sure. Leaving Kinvarra had nearly destroyed her. All this propinquity now only reopened old wounds that had hardly healed since. But what choice did she have?

Raising her head, she studied his striking face. The black eyes were veiled. His expression indicated impatience with her havering and no hint of amorous intent.

Of course there wasn't. He didn't want her. And nor, it seemed, did Harold. She'd been alone for so long. She'd never felt as alone as she did at this moment.

Alicia didn't try to hide her reluctance. "Very well."

Kinvarra's lips twitched at her lack of enthusiasm. "I'll tell the landlord that we'll take his last chamber."

Shock held her silent as she realized how much he'd changed. The man she'd married would have caviled at her unmannerly acceptance. Heavens, the man she'd married would have thrown a tantrum if she'd so much as glanced at another man, let alone eloped with him. Kinvarra hadn't just grown into his looks, he'd grown into his power.

He bowed briefly and strode away with a smooth, confident gait. As a youth, he'd been almost sinfully beautiful with his black hair and glittering eyes, but the man of thirty-two was formidable and in command of himself in a way his younger self had never been.

Alicia watched him go, wanting to turn away but unable to shift her gaze. What would she make of him if they met for the first time now? Honesty compelled her to acknowledge she would probably like him. She'd certainly notice him—no woman could ignore such a handsome man, with his air of authority and competence.

While admitting the fact made her skin itch with pique, she was glad Kinvarra had arrived to rescue her from that ditch. If she'd relied on Harold to solve their problems, she'd still be standing by the roadside.

Given the shambles downstairs, the bedchamber was

surprisingly clean and wonderfully snug to a woman shivering with cold. Silently Alicia removed her gloves, then slid her dripping red cloak from her shoulders, folded it and placed it on top of a carved wooden chest.

It seemed ridiculous to feel shy in the presence of the man she'd married eleven years ago, but she did. Across the room, Kinvarra removed his muddy outdoor clothes, revealing a plain blue coat and buff breeches.

A troupe of maids delivered hot water and a substantial supper, then disappeared, leaving Alicia standing in a bedroom with her husband for the first time in ten years.

She tried to ignore the massive tester bed in the corner. Out on the moors, she'd have scoffed at the idea of letting her husband touch her in passion, even if he wanted to. But with every moment in this room, a strange tension built between them, a tension that vibrated with desire long denied.

Did Kinvarra feel this tremulous awareness, too? Or was it all her imagination? Was he hoping to join her in that bed? And if he was, what would her response be?

Last week, yesterday, an hour ago, it would have been a contemptuous refusal.

Now? Now, she wasn't so sure what she wanted. She had an unwelcome inkling that she might want her husband.

She shivered, but whether with nerves or anticipation, she couldn't have said.

Kinvarra poured a glass of claret from the decanter on the sideboard. He took a mouthful, then turned to watch Alicia lower herself gingerly into an oak chair near the fire.

Frowning with concern, he strode toward her. "You told me you weren't hurt."

Again, that protective air. She fought to strangle the warmth curling in her heart. And failed. Heaven help her, she needed to remember the last time they'd been alone together, or she risked making an awful fool of herself.

She shook her head, even as she relished the blessed relief of sitting on something that didn't move. "I'm bruised, and stiff from cold and riding, but, no, I'm not hurt."

"You were lucky. The curricle is beyond repair. I know the road was icy, but the going wasn't hazardous, for all that. Was Henry driving too fast?"

"Perhaps." She paused before grudgingly admitting, "We were arguing."

"You? Arguing with a man?" Without shifting his gaze from her face, Kinvarra dropped to his knees before her. She guessed that he meant to help her remove her boots. It was an act familiar from their short intimacy, before everything went wrong. "I find that hard to believe."

"Shocking, isn't it?" Her lips curved upward in a reluctant smile, as she stared down into obsidian eyes alight with sardonic amusement.

Nobody else had ever teased her. Even Kinvarra when they'd lived together had been too intense at first, then too angry. To her surprise, she found she enjoyed his playfulness.

He'd been angry with her earlier, but she sensed no rage in him now. Instead, beneath his humor, he seemed watchful, waiting. Another anticipatory shiver rippled through her.

Kinvarra extended his glass, and she accepted it. His attention didn't waver from her face when she raised it to her lips. Heat bloomed inside her. From the wine, and from the unspoken intimacy of drinking from the place his lips had touched. It was almost like sharing a kiss.

Stop it, Alicia. You're letting the situation go to your head.

"What were you quarreling about?" Kinvarra asked, with an idleness that his grave attention contradicted.

She returned the glass, her hand slightly unsteady. "I decided I'd been reckless to take up Lord Harold's invitation to visit his hunting lodge. I was trying to get him to turn back to York."

She braced for gloating, a repeat of his triumphant reaction downstairs when he discovered she was still chaste. Kinvarra mightn't want her, but she'd always known he didn't want her sharing her body with anyone else either.

Her husband's regard held no smugness. How astonishing. "I'm glad to hear that," he said quietly.

She tried to sit up and scowl at him, summon one of the sharp-tongued responses that had come so easily out in the snow, but the effort was beyond her. Instead she tilted her head back against the chair. She closed her eyes, partly from weariness, partly because she flinched from reading messages that couldn't possibly be true in his dark, dark stare.

"He wasn't worthy of you, Alicia." Kinvarra's soft voice echoed in her heart, as did his use of her Christian name. He hadn't called her Alicia since the early days of their marriage, when they'd both still hoped to create something good from their union. "Why in God's name choose him of all men?"

Shock held her unmoving, as Kinvarra's bare hand slid over hers where it rested on the heavy arm of the chair. His palm was warm and slightly callused. Harold's hand had been softer than a woman's. She berated herself for making the comparison.

She opened her eyes and stared into her husband's face. Into the black eyes that for once appeared sincere and kind.

And she chanced an honest answer.

"I chose him because he was everything you are not, my lord."

Even more shocking than the touch of his hand, she watched him whiten under his tan. In all this time, she'd never realized that she had the power to hurt him. The knowledge pierced her like a blade, left her shaken.

He jerked back on his heels, removing his hand from hers. She tried not to miss that casual, comforting touch. The distance between them gaped like a chasm of ice.

"I...see." His voice firmed. "At least I'd never leave a woman alone to face down an angry husband, with a blizzard about to start."

Shamed heat stung her cheeks. She'd felt so strong and free and self-righteous when she'd arranged to go away with a lover. After ten barren years of thankless loyalty to a man who hardly cared she was alive.

But in retrospect, her behavior seemed shabby. Ill-advised. Despite her doubts, bravado and pride had kept her to her course until she'd reached York and that journey across the moors with no company but Harold and her howling conscience.

She'd fought against feeling guilty about betraying Kinvarra, but it was no use. It seemed her marriage vows still held her fast, despite her long misery. With every mile they'd covered, she'd become more convinced that succumbing to Harold's blandishments had been a horrible mistake.

Damn Kinvarra. He'd scarred her soul, and she'd never escape him.

"You wouldn't hurt me," she said with complete certainty.

"No, but Harold doesn't know that."

She noted that he was upset enough to use Harold's correct name. She tried to make light of the subject, but her voice emerged brittle and too high. "Anyway, no harm was done. I'm still the impossibly virtuous Countess of Kinvarra, who doesn't even sleep with her husband. You may rest easy in your bed, my lord, sure that your wife's reputation remains unblemished."

An emotion too complex for mere anger crossed his face, but his voice remained steady. "Why now, Alicia? What changed?"

"I was lonely." Her face still prickled with humiliation, and she knew from his expression that her shrug didn't convince. "I needed to do something to mark my permanent break from you. It was, in a way, our ten-year anniversary."

A muscle flickered in his cheek and his stare was uncompromising. "And you wanted to punish me."

Did she? Even after all this time, turbulent emotion swirled beneath their interactions. What amazed her was that they seemed finally capable of holding a conversation that wasn't composed entirely of spite and insults. Apparently they'd both changed in their years apart.

Alicia spoke with difficulty, even as she wondered why she confided in her husband of all people. When they'd lived together, he'd used any vulnerability as a weapon against her. "I haven't touched a man since I left you. I'm twenty-eight years old. I thought...I thought it was time I tested the waters again."

"With that cream puff?" He released a grunt of contemptuous laughter and made a slashing gesture with one hand. "If you're kicking over the traces, my girl, at least pick a man with blood in his veins."

"I've had a man with blood in his veins," she said in a low voice. "I didn't like it."

That couldn't be regret in his face, could it? One thing she remembered about Kinvarra was that he never accepted he was in the wrong. But when he spoke, he confounded her expectations.

"You had a selfish, impulsive boy in your bed, Alicia. Never mistake that."

Astonished, she stared at him kneeling before her. "When we parted, you blamed me for everything. You said touching me was…was like making love to a log of wood."

This time it was his turn to flush and glance away. "I'm sorry you recall that."

Even now, the snide remark made her flinch. Perhaps because there had been an element of truth in his sneer. "It was rather memorable."

When he looked back at her, she read remorse in his eyes. "No wonder you hated me."

She shrugged again, uncomfortable with the candid turn of the discussion. Because the agonizing truth was that she hadn't always hated him. Far from it. During most of their year together, she'd believed she loved him. And every nasty word he'd spoken had slashed her youthful heart to ribbons.

His unexpected honesty now forced her to recollect that she'd hardly been an angel in that particular argument. She'd called him a filthy, rutting animal and barred him from her bedroom.

Only now did she admit that he'd had provocation for his cruelty. And he'd been young, too. At the time, his four years seniority had seemed a lifetime. Now she realized he'd been a boy of twenty-one coping with a difficult wife, immature even for her seventeen years.

No wonder he'd been glad to see the back of her.

She struggled to swallow what felt like a boulder stuck in her throat. If they'd spoken like this after their marriage, perhaps they might have stayed together. But of course, neither of them had been capable of setting aside pride and vanity to face why their union failed. Now it was too late.

Too late—the saddest words in the language.

Her voice emerged as a husky whisper, and her hands tightened on the arms of the chair until they ached. "There's no point revisiting all this history. Really, tonight we're just chance-met strangers."

Kinvarra's lips tilted in the half-smile that had made her seventeen-year-old heart somersault. To her dismay, her mature self found the smile just as beguiling.

"Surely more than that." He raised his glass. "To my wife, the most beautiful woman I know."

"Stop it." Alicia turned away, blinking back hot tears. This excruciating weight of emotion in her chest was only weariness. She refused to recognize it as the knowledge that all those years ago she'd sacrificed something precious. "Tomorrow it will be as though this meeting never happened."

Even in her own ears, the words sounded choked with regret. She'd thought when she finally accepted Harold's advances that she was over her inconvenient yen for her husband. How tragically wrong she'd been. Tonight proved she was as impressionable as ever.

In silent defiance, she straightened her back against the chair. Kinvarra might be kind now, he might be considerate. But after all the pain between them, she could never let herself trust him again.

Kinvarra studied her with a speculative light in his black eyes. A premonitory shiver chilled her. If she wasn't careful, he'd have all her secrets. And she'd have no pride left.

She attempted a brighter tone. "Are you keeping that wine just for yourself?"

With a soft laugh, he raised his glass in another silent toast, as if awarding her a point in a contest. "Here."

He passed her the glass and bent to tug at her boot. She took a sip, hoping the claret would bolster her fortitude. It didn't.

Alicia hadn't missed the way Kinvarra leaned toward her as he spoke and the burgeoning tenderness in his manner. Nerves and unwilling arousal coiled in her stomach. Did he mean to attempt a seduction?

Although God knew why he'd be interested. If he'd

wanted her any time, he could have sent for her. His long silence spoke volumes about his indifference.

His hands were brisk and efficient, almost impersonal, as he pulled her boots off. Automatically she stretched her legs out and wriggled her toes. A relieved sigh escaped her.

As he sat back, he looked up with a smile. "Better?"

"Better," she admitted, taking some more wine. The rich flavor filled her mouth and slipped down her throat, washing away a little more of her bitterness.

Whatever happened tonight, she was unexpectedly grateful she'd had this chance to share a few hours with her husband. Hatred and rancor had dogged her since she'd left Kinvarra. Only now as those reactions ebbed did she realize how they'd soured her life. She inhaled, feeling as though she breathed fully for the first time in ten years.

He laid one elegant hand on her ankle. Even through the stocking, his touch burned. "You always had cold feet."

She closed her eyes. Imagine him remembering such a minor detail. Common sense dictated that she pull back, that she'd veered into dangerous territory. "I still do."

"I'll warm them up."

"Mmm."

She was so tired, and the cozy room and surprisingly cordial atmosphere sapped her will. When Kinvarra began to rub her feet, gentle warmth stole up her legs. If his touch even hinted at encroaching further, she'd stop him. But all he did was buff her feet until she was ready to purr with pleasure.

"Don't stop," she whispered, even when her feet glowed with heat, and he had to reach forward to rescue the empty wine glass from her loosening hand.

He laughed softly, and she struggled not to hear fondness in the sound. Kinvarra wasn't fond of her. He'd never been fond of her. Family arrangement had foisted her on him, an English heiress to fill the coffers of his Scottish earldom. Her abominable behavior during their year together had only confirmed his suspicions that he'd married a brat.

"Let's have our supper before it gets cold. You're exhausted."

She let him take her hand and raise her to her feet. Who would have thought so much touching was involved when they agreed to share this room? But she was in too much of a daze to protest, as he led her to the small table and slid a filled plate before her.

She was so tired that it hardly registered that Kinvarra acted the perfect companion. When she couldn't eat much of the hearty but simple fare, he summoned the maids to clear the room. Without her having to ask, he granted her privacy to prepare for bed. Although she was too weary to do much more than a quick cat wash. When Kinvarra returned from the corridor, she was already in bed, still wearing her clothes.

What happened now? Surely after all this time, he wouldn't demand his marital rights, whatever frail accord they'd established. Still, apprehension tightened her stomach, and she clutched the sheets to her chest like a nervous virgin.

He glanced across at her, black eyes enigmatic in the candlelight. Inevitably the moment reminded her of their wedding night. He'd been the perfect companion then, too. Her gentle knight, the beautiful earl her parents had chosen, the kind, smiling man who had made her laugh and blush and thrill with feelings she didn't recognize. And who had taken her body with a painful urgency that had left her hurt and bewildered and crying.

After that, no matter what he did, she turned rigid with fear when he came to her bed. After a couple of weeks, he'd stopped approaching her. After a couple of months, he'd stopped speaking to her, except to quarrel. After a year, she'd suggested they live apart, and he'd agreed without demur. Probably relieved to have his pestilential wife off his hands.

He'd left England almost immediately on a four-year grand tour. When next she saw him, he'd become a worldly, supercilious stranger who barely spared her a word, and the pattern for their rare future encounters was set. She stayed in London while he mostly managed his Scottish estates, hundreds of miles to the north. When she'd left him, even that distance didn't seem far enough. She'd never wanted to see him again.

Alicia had spent their separation convinced that she bore all the injury in their marriage. Now, tonight, she wasn't so sure that she was blameless for the disaster of their union.

She lowered her eyes and pleated the sheets with unsteady fingers. "Are you coming to bed?"

One eyebrow arched in mocking amusement. "Why, Lady Kinvarra, is that an invitation?"

Her color rose. How lowering to be a woman of twenty-eight and still blush like an adolescent.

"It's a cold night. You've had a hard ride. I trust you." Strangely, so quickly on top of her earlier uncertainty, it was true.

He released a short laugh and turned away. "More fool you."

Confused, she watched him set the big carved chair nearer to the fire. He undressed down to breeches and a loose white shirt. "It's only a few hours until dawn. I'll do quite well here, thank you."

She'd completely misunderstood him. Not for the first time, she thought with more of the stabbing regret that seemed her constant companion tonight.

When he'd first insisted they share a room, she'd wondered if he had some darker purpose. Some plan to take the wife who so profligately offered herself to another man. To teach her who was her master.

His actions now proved her wrong.

What did she expect? That he'd suddenly want her

after all this time? She was a fool. She'd always been a fool where Sebastian Sinclair was concerned.

The constriction returned to her throat, the constriction that felt alarmingly like tears. She lay back and forced herself to speak. "Goodnight, then."

"Goodnight, Alicia."

He blew out the candles, leaving only the glow of the fire. On edge and preternaturally aware of his every move, she listened to him settle. He tugged off his boots and drew his greatcoat over him for warmth. There was an odd, familiar intimacy in hearing the creak of the chair and his soft sigh as he extended his legs toward the flames.

Alicia stretched out. The bed was warm and soft, and the sheets smelled fresh. She was weary to the bone, but no matter how she wriggled, she couldn't find that one comfortable spot.

Recollections of the day tormented her. Harold's craven desertion, which should have been a considerably sharper blow than it was. If her original plans had eventuated, she'd now be lying in his arms.

She should resent his weakness, his absence, but all she felt was vast relief. Her mind dwelled instead on Kinvarra's unexpected gallantry. The fleeting moments of affinity in this room. The powerful memories of their life together, memories that tonight stirred poignant sadness, instead of turbulent resentment.

Kinvarra had turned the chair toward the hearth, and all she could see of him was a gold-limned black shape. He was so still, he could be asleep. But something told her he was as wide awake as she.

"My lord?" she whispered.

"Yes, Alicia?" he responded immediately. "Can't you sleep?"

"No."

Their voices were hushed, which was absurd as there was nobody to hear. The wind rattled the windowpanes, and a log cracked in the fireplace. He was right, the weather had worsened.

"Are you cold?"

"No."

"Hungry?"

"No."

"What is it, then, lass?" He sounded tender, and his Scottish burr was more marked than usual. When his emotions were engaged, traces of his Highland childhood softened his speech. She remembered that from their year together.

That hint of vulnerability made her brave. "Come and lie down beside me. You can't be comfortable in that chair."

He didn't shift. "No."

"Oh."

She huddled into the bed and drew the blankets up around her neck as if they could fend off the brutal truth. Hurt seared her like a branding iron. Of course he wouldn't share the bed. He hated her. How could she forget? Tonight he just played the gentleman to a lady in distress. He'd do the same for anyone. Just because Alicia was his wife didn't make her special. Nothing had changed.

When they'd first married, she'd attempted to establish a rapport between them during daylight hours, some trust that she could carry with her into the nights. But when she'd rebuffed him in bed, he'd rebuffed her during the day. He'd made it blatantly clear that he didn't want her childish adoration. He wanted a woman who could satisfy him between the sheets, not a silly little girl who froze into a block of ice the instant her husband touched her.

Alicia blinked back more of the tears that had so often verged close tonight. She'd wept enough over the Earl of Kinvarra. She'd wept enough tears to fill the deep, dark waters of Loch Varra that extended down the glen from Balmuir House, his ancestral home.

"Hell, Alicia, I'm sorry. Don't cry."

She opened her eyes and through the mist of tears saw he'd risen to watch her. The fire lent enough light to reveal that he appeared tormented and unsure. Nothing like the all-powerful earl.

"I'm not crying," she said in a thick voice. "I'm just tired."

His mouth lengthened at her unconvincing assertion. He reached out with one hand to clutch the back of the chair. "Go to sleep."

"I can't." She wondered why she didn't let him be, instead of courting further misery.

"Damn it, Alicia…"

The hand on the chair tightened until his knuckles shone white in the flickering firelight. Kinvarra's long, lean body was as taut as a violin string. Tension vibrated in the air.

"I'm not…I'm not attempting to seduce you," she said, and suddenly wondered whether that was the truth.

What in heaven's name was wrong with her? Surely she couldn't want to revisit the messy humiliations of her married life. Memories of those fumbling, painful encounters had tormented her since she'd left him.

He closed his eyes as if he was in agony. "I know. Dear God, I know." His chest rose as he sucked in a shuddering breath. He opened his eyes and stared at her, his gaze blazing across the distance between them. "But if I get into that bed, there's no way I'll keep my hands to myself. And I don't want to hurt you again. *I couldn't bear to hurt you again.*"

She was appalled to hear the naked pain in his voice. This wasn't the man she remembered. That man hadn't cared that his passion had frightened and bewildered his inexperienced bride.

This man sent excitement skittering through her veins and made her burn for his touch. She'd never felt like this. It was like balancing on the edge of a cliff over a wild sea. Dear God, was she likely to end up smashed on the rocks below? The answer didn't matter. It was too late for caution.

On unsteady arms, she raised herself against the headboard and drew in a breath to calm her rioting heartbeat. Another breath. She took the last rash step into infinity.

Her voice was quiet but steady. "Then be gentle, Sebastian."

CHAPTER THREE

Kinvarra's grip on the chair turned punishing. Good God, he must be mistaken in what he'd heard. Alicia couldn't be offering herself. In all these many years, she'd never offered herself. Even in the beginning, he'd always had to take. He'd grown to hate it, whatever physical pleasure he found in her arms. When she'd finally begged for a separation after those wretched months together, he'd almost been relieved.

Of course, he hadn't realized then that his agreement would lead to ten excruciating years without his wife.

She sat up against the bedhead, pale against the dark wood, and watched him with a glow in her blue eyes that with any other woman he'd read as blatant sexual interest. She'd taken her beautiful golden hair down and it flowed around her shoulders, catching the firelight.

She'd become his fantasy Alicia. The unforgettable woman who had haunted every empty day he'd endured without her. The woman she'd never been for him, even when they lived together.

"Sebastian?" A faint frown drew her fine eyebrows together.

He should say something. His continuing silence must make her nervous.

"You don't know what you're asking," he said in a constricted voice, wondering why the hell he tried to talk her out of fulfilling his dearest hopes.

He'd missed Alicia since the day she left him. Now she was near enough to touch. And for once she didn't seem to loathe him. All his dearest, most outlandish hopes came to fruition. He'd always been blackguard enough to want more from their meeting tonight than mere conversation. One bed and a cold night and Alicia in an uncharacteristically amiable mood all seemed to augur at the very least a physical respite from his damnable longing.

Then he'd remembered those fraught encounters at Balmuir House. However much he wanted her, he couldn't face having to inflict himself upon her again. So he'd consigned himself to an excruciating night in the chair. That was less excruciating than seeing her now and knowing that she'd accept him into her bed—

and realizing that in his desperation, he was only too likely to disgust and frighten her again.

She raised her chin, an act of bravado familiar in the young Alicia. The memory made his gut clench with poignant yearning. He'd hurt her before. He couldn't bear to hurt her again. He must stay away from her, for both their sakes.

An uncertain smile curved her lips, as the silence extended into awkwardness. "Tonight you chased my lover away. Honor compels you to offer recompense." Then in a low voice, "Sebastian, once long ago, you wanted me. I know you did."

He swallowed and forced his response from a tight throat. "I still do."

She raised trembling hands to the buttons on her mannish ensemble. An ensemble that looked anything but mannish on her lush figure. She'd filled out from the girl he'd married. Delightfully so.

Her traveling garb was cut like a riding habit, and the white shirt under the dark jacket was suitably modest, buttoned high at the throat. Even so, when her fumbling fingers loosened that top button to reveal a couple of inches of skin, every drop of moisture dried from his mouth and his heart flung itself against his ribs.

The Earl of Kinvarra was accounted a brave man. But he immediately recognized the emotion holding him paralyzed as ice-cold fear.

Tonight provided a miraculous second chance to heal the breach in his marriage. A gift of love for Christmas Eve. But if he hurt Alicia again, he'd never have another opportunity to bring her back to him.

He needed patience, self-command, insight to seduce his wife into pleasure. Yet he burned hotter than a devil in hell.

What was he to do? He wanted her too much. And wanting her too much would destroy the cobweb of intimacy building between them in this quiet room. An intimacy woven from soft conversation and new understanding.

When his family had presented him with such a beautiful bride just after his twenty-first birthday, he'd been confident that he and Alicia would find happiness. Instead every coupling had been furtive and soured with shame, accomplished in darkness and ending with his wife sobbing into the pillow. No wonder he'd lost his taste for doing his marital duty, although to his endless torment, his desire had never waned.

Desire still roared inside him.

Her shirt fell open another fraction to show a delicate line of collarbone and a shadowy hint of her breasts. Her stare unwavering, her hand dropped to the next button.

"Stop," he said hoarsely.

Her hand paused in its downward progress.

"Stop?" The self-consciousness that flooded her face carved a rift in his heart. "You said—"

Shaking his head, he finally released the chair. He flexed his fingers to restore the blood flow. "And I meant it. But let's do this properly."

Her hand fell away from her shirt to lie loose in her lap. "Shouldn't I take my clothes off?"

Dear God, she was going to kill him before she was done.

Kinvarra closed his eyes and prayed for control as recollections of touching Alicia's naked body crammed into his mind and turned him as hard as an oak staff. When he opened them, she watched him as if he acted like a madman. She wasn't far wrong.

"We've got plenty of time." He stepped toward the bed, his hands opening and closing at his sides as he fought the urge to seize her and tumble her back against the mattress. "Why rush things?"

"Kinvarra…" she said unsteadily.

She might have invited his attentions, but he caught the flash of trepidation in her eyes. He didn't underestimate the courage she'd needed to ask him to join her.

"You called me Sebastian before."

"You weren't staring at me as if you wanted to eat me then." She clutched at the sheet although she didn't pull it higher. He was close enough now to notice the wild flutter of her pulse at her delicate throat and the way her erratic breathing made her swelling breasts rise and fall.

"Believe me, I'd love to." The urge to rush, to grab,

to possess before she changed her mind thundered in his veins, but he resisted its demands. He had to rein himself in, or the promise of joy would disintegrate to dust.

Her scent washed over him, floral soap and something honeyed and enticing that was the essence of Alicia. In all this time, he'd never forgotten. He drew a deep breath, taking that delicious fragrance deep into his lungs.

Slowly, as if any untoward movement might scare her away, he reached for the hand that crushed the sheet. At the contact, she jerked and released a choked gasp.

"Don't be afraid, Alicia," he murmured, feeling her trembling in his grasp. "I won't hurt you."

He hoped to hell he spoke true. His grip tightened, even as he told himself he needed to be careful with her.

"I'm…I'm not afraid," she said on a thread of sound.

He laughed softly and lowered himself to sit on the bed, his hip resting against the blankets over her legs. "Liar."

She blushed. As a girl, her blushes had charmed him. They still did, he discovered.

"I'm nervous. That's not the same as afraid."

Kinvarra raised her hand to his lips and kissed it. He felt her shiver, and unmistakable response darkened her eyes. Turning her hand over, he kissed her palm. When he heard her breath catch, desire spurred him to take more, satisfy his pounding need. With difficulty he beat back his arousal.

She remembered him as a selfish lover. He needed to vanquish those bleak memories and replace them with bliss. His voice deepened into sincerity. "Alicia, trust me."

His gaze held hers. Doubt, fear, and something that might have been reluctant hope swirled in her eyes. He felt tension in the hand he held.

In aching suspense, he waited for her to agree. Surely she couldn't be so merciless as to deny him now.

The silence extended. And extended.

Then finally, *finally,* she nodded.

"I trust you, Sebastian."

Relief flooded him, made him dizzy. Relief and gratitude. After the mull he'd made of everything, he didn't deserve her consent, but he was bloody glad she'd given it all the same.

Now he had it, he'd make sure she never regretted it.

"Thank you," he whispered, wondering if she knew how profoundly he meant those simple words.

He leaned forward to brush his lips across hers. A deliberately light kiss, however much her nearness eviscerated good intentions. A glancing touch that promised more. A salute to the woman who tonight would become his partner in rapture.

Her lips were impossibly soft under his. Smooth. Satiny. He lingered a second, savoring the exquisite sensation. In nearly eleven years, he hadn't kissed his wife. He'd kissed her before they'd married, during the giddy days of their short engagement. He'd kissed her during their first weeks together, but the spiraling unhappiness of their life at Balmuir had soon made kissing seem a travesty.

Kinvarra started to withdraw, the beast inside him straining against gentleness. Then Alicia made a soft sound deep in her throat and her lips parted.

Her warm breath filled his mouth. She tasted familiar. Yet as fresh and new as a fall of snow. Hot darkness exploded inside his head, and reaction ripped through him. He longed to ravish her mouth with all the passion locked for so long inside him. Struggling to remember what was at stake, he clenched his hands in the blankets.

God give him strength. His control already shredded, and he'd hardly launched his seduction.

Alicia cradled his head between her hands, holding him close, as though afraid he meant to pull away, even now. Foolish woman, as if he was going anywhere. He'd ventured up to the gates of paradise, and to his astonishment, they'd opened to allow him inside.

Her kiss was clumsy, as if she hadn't kissed anyone in a long time. Shock rocketed through him. On an intellectual level, he'd known that she'd never been unfaithful. But that urgent, unpracticed kiss reassured his needy soul that in all the years they'd been apart, she'd belonged only to him.

Once, when he'd been an arrogant stripling who believed the world was his for the taking, that knowledge might have provoked triumph. Now he was only humbly grateful that she'd waited for him.

After so long without her, he took nothing for granted. He was under no illusions how lucky he was that Alicia was in his arms right now. The slightest misstep could put them at odds again. This time forever.

His arms encircled her, curved her into his body. She molded to him with an eagerness that set his heart cartwheeling. His mouth shaped itself to hers as she curled her arms around his neck. Her breasts crushed into his chest, until blazing heat threatened to incinerate all will beyond his hunger to possess. Even as he kissed her deeply, ravenously, stroking her tongue with his, he struggled to remember that he couldn't dive headlong into this fire.

Kinvarra's resolution faltered when her tongue moved in unmistakable response and she moaned with female pleasure. Restraint became even shakier after she sighed into his mouth and rubbed her body against his.

His shaking hands clasped her head as he plundered her mouth, stoking her passion. She began to touch him, feverish brushes of her hands, as if after all this time she needed to learn the shape of his body again.

Her unfettered reactions intoxicated him. Who would have guessed his wife contained such delicious wildness? She was glorious, the answer to his every dream. When he finally raised his head, she whimpered in protest and her eyes were dark and slumberous under heavy, drooping eyelids.

A soft, shaken laugh escaped him as he stroked his hands through the soft hair at her temples. He couldn't resist touching her—he couldn't rely on fate being generous enough to let her stay with him past tonight. "I'm struggling to be careful, my darling, but you make it almost impossible."

Uneven gasps escaped her moist, parted lips. Her face was flushed with arousal.

"I'm not seventeen anymore, Sebastian," she whispered. "I won't break."

Almost reverently, he cupped her jaw. "You deserve respect."

Her smile was tremulous. "Is that what you feel for me?"

"Of course," he said swiftly. Then after a pause, "And desire."

"Show me the desire."

He bit back an agonized groan. Reining in his hunger was the most fiendish of tortures. But she couldn't know what she asked. He'd acted the savage with her when he'd been a mere boy, but now he wanted her with a man's passion. If she'd thought him a barbarian then, she'd quail if he unleashed the fierce hunger raging inside him tonight.

"I promised I wouldn't hurt you," he said in a raw tone.

Her gaze was steady. "You won't."

"I did once." Shame bit deep, chastened his craving, although nothing could ease his craving apart from having her. The devil of it was that one night, however dazzling, would never be enough for him.

She touched his cheek with a tenderness that speared him with guilty awareness of how badly he'd behaved. "We've both grown up since then, Sebastian. I trust you. Please, trust yourself."

Staring into her beautiful face, Kinvarra realized she was right. She was no longer the frightened girl he'd first married, and he was no longer the greedy, thoughtless boy too callow to appreciate the jewel that fate had delivered into his keeping.

The yearning to prove himself worthy of her confidence flooded him. He couldn't fail her now. But nor could he continue to treat her as if she were made of spun glass. It would destroy him.

Time had changed them, and now it offered the opportunity to start again, to move beyond their mistakes and create something new and invincible and shining. He wanted to insist on declarations, but he was wise enough to know that the moment was too fragile to bear the weight of anything beyond the present.

As he undid the next button on her shirt, his hands were gentle. By the time he slid the garment from her shoulders and let it fall to the floor, she was trembling. Her hands had dropped to her sides.

Her scent filled his head, making him drunk with desire. Even so, he still held back. Painful as restraint was. Carefully he undressed her. Finally she was bare to his sight, and he paused in wonder.

In their years apart, she'd changed. Her body was a woman's. Ripe. Alluring.

He drew a shuddering breath and reminded himself of the risks in what he did. His blood beat hot and hard, but he managed to cling to control.

Just.

In shy wantonness, Alicia lay spread before him. Color lined her slanted cheekbones, and the breath came fast between her lips. Almost hesitantly, Kinvarra reached out to cup one full, white breast. It plumped in his hand as if created for his touch, and the raspberry nipple pearled.

When he bent to kiss that impudent peak, Alicia's surprised gasp of pleasure rewarded him. He drew harder on the nipple and ran his hand down the smooth plain of her belly to the feathery curls at the juncture of her thighs.

She was already damp. Her musky scent lay heavy on the air. This slow seduction worked its magic on his wife, too. He took her other nipple between his lips and bit softly at the crest. She shifted restlessly under his hand and buried her fingers in his hair, urging him to continue.

He needed no further encouragement. But as he licked and bit and suckled, as his hands roamed her silky skin, some trace of reason lingered. She wasn't ready yet, however her touch and sighs spurred him to further depredations.

He wanted to be inside her more than he wanted his next breath. But this night wasn't about what he wanted, but about showing her the pleasure a man and a woman could find together. To his everlasting regret, he'd never given her that.

Her mouth kept luring him back. He had ten years of kisses to make up for. Each kiss was hotter and sweeter than the last. He couldn't get enough of her taste.

"You're wearing too many clothes," she said in a broken voice.

"Whereas you're dressed just right," he said with a low laugh, kissing her breast again.

She'd been lovely as a girl, fresh and dewy and as rich with promise as a furled rose. But now the voluptuous woman in his arms took his breath away.

With every second, he felt her confidence increase. When she dragged his shirt up from his breeches, her caresses on his naked back shot lightning behind his eyes.

"Sebastian, I want to see you."

He'd never heard her sound like this, choked and frantic and starving for him. In those joyless, mean little encounters in his bed at Balmuir House, she hadn't spoken at all. And then she'd cried. This woman claimed her right to sample every pleasure.

He couldn't remain immune to her pleading. He rolled off the bed and tore his clothes away, hurling them into the corner. Then he paused, wondering if he should have been more circumspect. Would his rampant nakedness terrify his wife?

When she was a girl, his unabashed maleness had frightened her. He'd come to her in the dark, and even then what he'd done had revolted her. Could that have changed?

She slid up against the headboard, making no pretense at modesty by covering herself with the sheet. Dear Lord, she was a sight to set a man's passions afire. Her face was flushed with eagerness and curiosity, her lips were full and red, her body was a symphony of curves and hollows. Her golden hair cascaded around her shoulders, teasingly covering one breast and leaving the other bare. Kinvarra felt himself grow harder, larger, needier.

Her eyes widened as her inspection continued down past his chest and belly. Hell, what would he do if she stopped him now?

Could he stop?

Yes, something inside him insisted. For Alicia, he could stop.

"Magnificent," she murmured, her eyes glinting blue fire under their heavy lids.

Her smile glowed with such anticipation that his

foolish heart crashed inside his chest. She'd always been able to confound him with a mere word. A decade without her hadn't changed that.

She stretched out one hand in invitation. To his astonishment, she wasn't shaking. All trace of her earlier uncertainty had vanished.

"Come to me, my husband."

CHAPTER FOUR

Alicia studied the expressions that flitted across Sebastian's striking face. Somewhere in the last years, perhaps only since they'd entered this room and laid down their weapons against each other, she'd learned to read him. When they'd first married, she hadn't known how to pierce his shell of physical perfection to reach the man beneath. He'd seemed a godlike creature, too far above lowly mortals for her to feel worthy of being his wife.

But the man who stood before her, superb in his nakedness, was heartbreakingly human.

For all his strength and beauty, he was vulnerable. Even more, he was vulnerable to her. She'd always felt powerless in this marriage. Now she recognized his overwhelming longing for her. And with a shock, realized that he'd longed for her when they'd first married, too. How had she never seen that before?

Tonight she'd also learned that he blamed himself for their difficulties. How odd, when finally she admitted that she'd been at least as much at fault as he. She'd been over-indulged, demanding, headstrong, quick to take umbrage, slow to offer understanding or tolerance.

Tonight she surveyed her husband's powerful body and rejoiced in a woman's desire. And a woman's ability to forgive. She'd finally cast away the chains of hatred and prejudice. Sensual need raged in her blood, made her heart pump with eagerness to know this man's possession. Fear was present as well, but she refused to succumb to it. Fear had crippled her for far too long.

She saw also that he was still unsure of her, unaware how much she'd changed. He didn't know that, after a long and difficult road, she'd discovered exactly where she ought to be.

In Kinvarra's arms. Forever.

How had she ever imagined that weak, inadequate Harold Fenton could compare with the wonderful man she'd married?

"Sebastian, I want you," she said softly, surprised at how easily the words emerged. "Don't make me wait."

Something in her voice or her smile must have convinced him she'd grown beyond the skittish girl who had fled his passion. Determination lit his face, hardened his jaw, set his eyes glinting in a way that, for all her arousal, made her pulse race with apprehension.

And excitement.

How had she never understood what an exciting man she'd married? The seventeen-year-old Alicia must have been blind. And insane.

This was no time for regrets. Not when her tall, handsome, overwhelmingly virile husband prowled toward her with such purpose. He betrayed none of his earlier reticence in the way he drew her into his arms and tugged her under him. There was just hunger and a masculine strength that made her feel both delicate as a lily and stronger than steel.

She thought she'd measured his passion in his kisses. But now he was insatiable. He touched her everywhere, kissing her as if he couldn't get enough of her mouth, whispering praise until she trembled with delight.

He touched her between her legs, stroking the sleek folds. She shuddered against him as frenzied response flared. New, strange, astonishing pleasure. She cried out his name and jerked her hips up to meet him.

Alicia wanted him to take her, to fill the lonely reaches of her soul, to feed her starving senses. Her arms closed hard around him, feeling the coil and release of the muscles in his back as he moved over her.

He rose above her, caging her between his arms, and she caught the turbulent emotion in his face as he stared down into her face. The moment spun into eternity, then shattered when with a single commanding thrust, he joined his body to hers.

Her muscles tightened in instinctive protest at his powerful possession. After the years without him, the invasion felt unfamiliar, uncomfortable. He was a large man, and she'd been chaste for so long. She dragged in a shuddering breath, struggling to adjust to his size and vigor.

Another breath, heavy with Sebastian's musky, male essence. She shifted, angled her hips, felt him slide further inside her. Then magically all awkwardness flowed away, and with perfect naturalness, she arched up to join him in a union as much of soul as of body.

And recognized with despairing clarity that she'd never stopped loving him.

Her fingers curled into the hot, bare skin of his shoulders as the inexorable truth rolled over her like a huge wave. Then she closed her eyes and gave herself up to Sebastian.

Right now he was hers. She refused to let the old, unsure Alicia ruin this ultimate closeness. Her body clenched around him in a silent plea to stay with her, never to leave.

She felt his tension as he held himself still, then with hard, purposeful strokes that built her arousal to an inferno, he began to move. The dance wasn't new to her, although the radiant intimacy was.

Alicia soared higher and higher until she touched the burning sky. She shook and sighed and clung to him, blind to everything but the rising tension inside her. This was beyond anything she'd ever felt. Beyond anything she'd even imagined.

At the peak, glittering light blinded her and she cried out. Such fierce ecstasy. Such glory.

Such love.

Vaguely through the swirling storm of passion, she heard Sebastian's deep groan. He shuddered and plunged deep, spilling liquid heat inside her. For a long moment, he held himself taut before he slumped over her, his body heavy with satisfaction.

Alicia lay in a haze of physical sensation. So this was what a man's possession could be. She'd been a wife for eleven years, yet she'd had no idea. No idea at all what she'd missed.

The air was redolent of their lovemaking. It was as if she breathed the memory of pleasure. She tightened her grip on Sebastian's back, feeling the sinews flex as he settled himself against her without withdrawing. She'd never felt so close to another person. For the first time in her life, she felt whole.

The fire burned low, leaving the room in twilight. Alicia stared up at the ceiling, watching the shadows gather. Nothing could dull the glow she felt. She felt made anew. She felt capable of conquering the world. She felt tired and languorous and ready to sleep for a week. Maintaining the long pretense that she cared nothing for her husband had exhausted her, like a huge weight dragging behind her wherever she went.

Right now, she felt lighter than air. Free. Fulfilled.

With sudden desperation, her fingers dug into his back. Oh, dear heaven, don't let fate take Sebastian away, not now that she'd discovered him again. Not now that she was finally woman enough to be his wife in every sense.

He'd undoubtedly wanted her when he'd taken her. Not even the most inexperienced woman could have assumed otherwise.

But had Sebastian intended this night to be a last goodbye to an unhappy past? Or had they taken the first step in a long, joyful journey together?

Kinvarra gasped for breath, his heartbeat drumming wildly in his ears. An ocean of satisfaction flooded his body, even as he cursed himself for losing control. He'd planned to take his time, prepare Alicia, raise her to peak after peak before he sought his own relief. But when he'd touched his wife's naked body and read desire in her shining eyes, he hadn't been able to hold back.

He'd been hungry, even hungrier than he'd been as an eager boy, although at least this time, praise the angels, she hadn't closed away from him in fear. Instead she'd achieved her own delight in his arms. He'd felt the way she tightened, milking him, and he hadn't mistaken her broken cry as she'd arched to take him deep in the final moments.

His big body still pressed her into the mattress. She must feel crushed, suffocated. He was a swine not to shift away.

But how sweet it was to lie here in the aftermath, to let his hands wander her silky skin, to listen to the soft music of her breathing, to rest surrounded by Alicia.

Heaven couldn't offer an eternity of bliss purer than this moment.

Making love to his wife offered a profundity of experience he'd never known. He'd grieve forever if this was the sum of happiness allotted to him. If he was to possess her only this once.

Tonight they'd moved from hostility through a brittle trust to a conflagration of rapture. But was this truce only a pause in ongoing warfare? Or could it form the foundations of a life together?

He prayed so, but years of futile yearning had taught him not to rely on the promise of happiness.

Just like that, reality descended. He and Alicia had enjoyed blazing pleasure tonight, but it didn't answer the larger questions. He needed her commitment beyond one tumble between the sheets, no matter how earth-shaking that tumble was.

He'd wanted this woman since he'd first seen her. And as more than his lover, however powerful his desire. He wanted to know her as the other half of his spirit. He wanted to build a family with her. He wanted to grow old at her side. Nothing in ten years of separation had changed that.

But he was wise enough now to know that wanting wasn't enough.

He could probably compel her to return to him. After all, the law was on his side. But for all his faults, he'd never been a bully. And he couldn't bear to have her hating him again. He'd glimpsed something in her eyes tonight that had set his heart dancing. Although after being hurt for so long, it was impossible to be sure.

Could he face letting her go, if she rose from this bed and announced she went back to London alone?

He might not be a bully, but the primitive who skulked inside him howled denial at the prospect of losing her again.

Slowly he raised himself on his elbows to stare down at her. He smoothed the disheveled blond hair away from her face. She looked beautiful, replete, weary. In spite of his good intentions, he'd used her ruthlessly. He'd wanted to cherish her, but passion had swept them up into a whirlwind where all that mattered was the drive to blinding consummation.

Piercing tenderness overwhelmed him, and he bent his head to kiss her gently on the lips. Not the hard, demanding kisses of earlier, although the ghost of his hunger lingered in the soft touch. "Are you all right?"

She smiled up at him, and he struggled against believing that the light in her eyes was love. "Better than all right." Her slender throat worked as she swallowed. "That was…that was remarkable."

"Yes." He fought against saying more. She was tired and defenseless. It wasn't fair just now to harangue her about the future. Instead he kissed her again then rolled to the side. "It's nearly morning."

"Mmm."

When he drew her against his side, she was slack with exhaustion, a delicious bundle of warm, sated womanhood. He paused to savor the moment, praying again that it spoke of a new start and not an ending. He'd sell his soul for the chance to hold her like this for the rest of their lives.

Kinvarra held his wife until she slept, but for all his weariness and the throb of sexual satisfaction through his body, he couldn't settle. Eventually he rose and padded over to the window. Now that the fire had burned down to ashes, the morning air was cold on his bare skin.

Very quietly so as not to wake Alicia, he parted the curtains. Immediately brilliant light flooded the room. It was later than he'd realized. The storm had blown itself out overnight, and the pale sun rose over the horizon, painting the fresh snow gold and making it sparkle like diamonds.

The idyll of a winter's night had given way to a new day. Christmas Day, he realized with surprise. A day of hope fulfilled. A day of beginnings.

Just what would those beginnings bring?

Would his glimpse of paradise prove brutally brief? Could all the lovely harmony of these last hours crash on the rocks of past wrongs and his insatiable demands?

Heaven forgive him, but he didn't know how to be anything but demanding. He wanted Alicia with him. He wanted her in his bed. He couldn't stop himself.

He'd spent ten years yearning for her from afar. The experience had devastated him. He couldn't go back to that again.

He mightn't have any choice, damn it.

"How beautiful."

Kinvarra had been so lost in his troubled thoughts, he hadn't heard Alicia rise from the bed. His heart slammed to a stop as she slid her arms around his waist and pressed her warmth into his back. He curled his hands over the windowsill to stop himself from sweeping her up and carrying her back to bed.

The bright light of Christmas Day told him that the magical night was over. Too soon, too soon, his aching heart protested. Now he'd tasted her ardor, he couldn't live without her. And she'd tempted him with more than passion. The sweet intimacy of last night's conversation. The tenderness of her embrace now.

Alicia was everything he wanted. Enduring their separation had been difficult enough before he'd glimpsed this joy. Now if she meant to leave him again, she'd destroy him.

"I thought you were asleep," he said softly.

"I missed you."

His gut lurched with anguish as she brushed a kiss

across his bare shoulder. "I've missed you every day," he said before he could stop himself.

"I thought you were glad to be rid of me." Her voice was muffled against his skin. "I can't blame you. I was such a silly chit."

"You were enchanting. You still are."

"You didn't think so at the time." The sheer neutrality of her tone betrayed her suffering as nothing else could.

He swallowed the choking lump in his throat and admitted the humiliating truth. "Yes, I did. But I believed the world would bend to my will merely for the asking. You were too fine for my possessing, and I was too arrogant to see just what a treasure I had. I was impatient and self-centered, and you were right to hate me."

"You weren't impatient last night."

He laughed without amusement. "Misery is an excellent schoolmaster. I've learned the error of my ways. Although I can't expect you to believe that, after the hash I've made of everything."

"I should have trusted you." Her voice was muffled.

"I wasn't worthy of your trust then."

The question hovered—was he worthy of her trust now? He prayed desperately that it was so. He prayed that he hadn't placed himself beyond redemption and that she'd give him another chance.

Kinvarra wanted to swear his allegiance, promise he'd never hurt her again, vow to make her happy. But emotion too strong for words jammed the declarations in his throat.

Silence fell, a silence heavy with remembered pain and everything still unspoken between them. Because he couldn't resist touching her, he rested his hands lightly on hers. The urge stirred to seize, to grab, to compel, but he crushed it.

Last night, she'd given herself freely. He refused to compromise that memory. After today, it might be all he had left.

She sighed softly, her breath a sensual tickle against his skin. "The snow is so clean." Her voice was soft, musing. As if she spoke to herself rather than for his ears. "Even after the storm, it's perfect. It's waiting for us to make the first footprints."

He tightened his grip on her hands. So much hinged on the next moments. He struggled to find the right words, wondering if the right words even existed.

"Our future could be like that, Alicia. A new path. A new life. A Christmas miracle." He paused, swallowed, and his voice was husky when he spoke what lay in his heart. "Come back to me."

He felt her stiffen. His heart breaking, he waited for her to move away, to reject him, to speak in that cold, cutting tone that she'd reserved for their few meetings in London.

"For how long?" Her voice was quiet.

She hadn't moved away. Yet.

Kinvarra stared at the glittering scene outside

without seeing it. Instead he remained utterly focused on his wife. Again, he risked honesty, even if honesty cost him all hope of achieving his dream.

"For the rest of our lives."

This time she did draw away, and he felt the inches between them as grim absence. "Why?"

He turned to study her. The light from the window illuminated her as if she stood on a stage. Swathed in the white bed sheet, she looked unhappy and uncertain and remarkably young. Almost as young as the pretty girl he'd married. "Because I love you."

"No…" She shook her head in disbelief.

Kinvarra smiled at her, even while she split his heart into a hundred bleeding pieces. Again. "Yes."

Alicia raised her chin and regarded him as if what he said made no sense. "I was so foul to you. How can you ever forgive me?"

"How can you forgive *me*? Let's rise above the past, my darling. I want you with me. I've never wanted anything else. Don't let old mistakes destroy our hope of happiness." He paused and swallowed. "If you love me, come back to me."

For an unendurable moment, her expression didn't change. Kinvarra's every heartbeat tolled the knell of doom. Then the tension drained from her face, and her eyes turned as blue as a clear sky. Suddenly, in the depths of winter, he basked in the reviving warmth of summer sunlight.

Alicia stepped toward him, although she didn't

touch him. "Sebastian, I love you, too. We've wasted so much time. Let's not waste any more."

Shaking, he reached out to curl his hands around her upper arms and drag her unresisting body against him. He could hardly believe that this was happening. Yesterday he'd been lost in an eternal mire of despair. Today the world offered love and hope, and a future with the woman he adored. The swiftness of the change was dizzying, left him reeling.

"My wife," he murmured and kissed her with all the reverence he felt when he spoke those two words. "My countess. My beloved."

The vivid, passionate woman in his arms kissed him back with a fervor that set his blood rushing in a wild torrent. Bright, unfamiliar joy flooded him as he realized that Alicia at last was his.

Then because it was cold, and he wanted her, and he loved her—and he'd been apart from her for longer than mortal man could bear—Kinvarra swung his smiling wife up in his arms and strode across to the rumpled bed.

ABOUT THE AUTHOR

ANNA CAMPBELL has written 10 multi award-winning historical romances for Grand Central Publishing and Avon HarperCollins, and her work is published in 22 languages. She has also written 23 bestselling independently published romances, including her series, The Dashing Widows and The Lairds Most Likely. Anna has won numerous awards for her Regency-set stories including Romantic Times Reviewers Choice, the Booksellers Best, the Golden Quill (three times), the Heart of Excellence (twice), the Write Touch, the Aspen Gold (twice) and the Australian Romance Readers Association's favorite historical romance (five times). Her books have three times been nominated for Romance Writers of America's presti-gious RITA Award, and three times for Australia's Romantic Book of the Year. When she's not traveling the world seeking inspiration for her stories, Anna lives on the beautiful east coast of Australia.

Anna loves to hear from her readers. You can find her at:

Website: www.annacampbell.com

facebook.com/AnnaCampbellFans

twitter.com/AnnaCampbellOz

bookbub.com/authors/anna-campbell

goodreads.com/AnnaCampbell

ALSO BY ANNA CAMPBELL

Claiming the Courtesan

Untouched

Tempt the Devil

Captive of Sin

My Reckless Surrender

Midnight's Wild Passion

The Sons of Sin series:

Seven Nights in a Rogue's Bed

Days of Rakes and Roses

A Rake's Midnight Kiss

What a Duke Dares

A Scoundrel by Moonlight

Three Proposals and a Scandal

The Dashing Widows:

The Seduction of Lord Stone

Tempting Mr. Townsend

Winning Lord West

Pursuing Lord Pascal

Charming Sir Charles

Catching Captain Nash

Lord Garson's Bride

The Lairds Most Likely:

The Laird's Willful Lass

The Laird's Christmas Kiss

The Highlander's Lost Lady

The Highlander's Defiant Captive

The Highlander's Christmas Quest

Christmas Stories:

The Winter Wife

Her Christmas Earl

A Pirate for Christmas

Mistletoe and the Major

A Match Made in Mistletoe

The Christmas Stranger

Other Books:

These Haunted Hearts

Stranded with the Scottish Earl

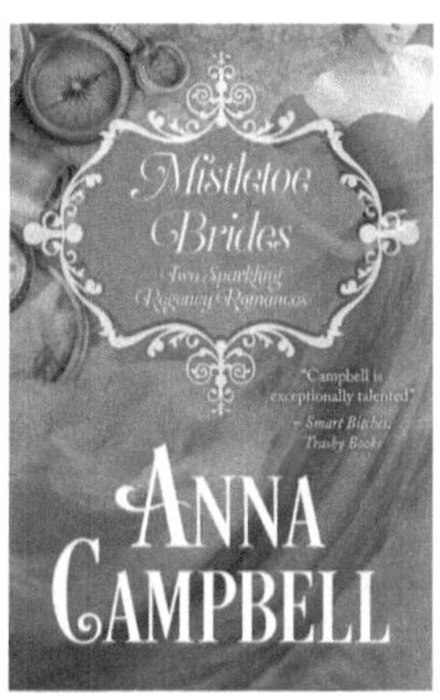

Her Christmas Earl

No good deed goes unpunished...

To save her hen-witted sister from scandal, Philippa Sanders ventures into a rake's bedroom – and into his power. Now her reputation hangs by a thread and only a hurried marriage can rescue her. Is the Earl of Erskine the heartless libertine the world believes? Or will Philippa discover unexpected honor in a man notorious for his wild ways?

Blair Hume, the dissolute Earl of Erskine, has had his eye on the intriguing Miss Sanders since he arrived at this deadly dull house party. Now a reckless act delivers this beguiling woman into his hands as a delightful Christmas gift. Is fate offering him a fleeting Yuletide diversion? Or will this Christmas Eve encounter spark a passion that lasts a lifetime?

A Pirate for Christmas

Pursued by the pirate...

Bess Farrar might be an innocent village miss, but she knows enough about the world to doubt Lord Channing's motives when he kisses her the very day they meet. After all, local gossip insists that before this dashing rake became an earl, he sailed the Seven Seas as a ruthless pirate.

Bewitched by the vicar's daughter...

Until he unexpectedly inherits a title, staunchly honorable Scotsman Rory Beaton has devoted his adventurous life to the Royal Navy. But he sets his course for tempestuous new waters when he meets lovely, sparkling Bess Farrar. Now this daring mariner will do whatever it takes to convince the spirited lassie to launch herself into his arms and set sail into the sunset.

A Christmas marked by mayhem.

Wooing his vivacious lady, the new Earl of Channing finds himself embroiled with matchmaking villagers, an eccentric vicar, mistaken identities, a snowstorm, scandal, and a rascally donkey. Life at sea was never this exciting. The gallant naval captain's first landlocked Christmas promises hijinks, danger, and passion – and a breathtaking chance to win the love of a lifetime.

Kisses and Christmas Bells

Two Romantic Regency Novellas

Mistletoe and the Major

The Major is home from the wars at last...

Edmund Sherritt, Major Lord Canforth, has devoted eight tumultuous years to fighting Napoleon. Finally Europe is at peace, and he can retire to his estates and the lovely wife he hasn't seen since their brief, unhappy honeymoon. The innocent girl he loved from the first moment he saw her, but who shied away from him on their wedding night.

The beautiful woman who greets him at Otway Hall on Christmas Eve is no longer the sweet ingénue he remembers. This new and exciting version of his beloved countess is strong, outspoken, and independent, and she's willing to stand up for what she wants. The question is—does she want the husband who returns to her arms more as a stranger than a spouse?

Now the real battle begins.

Felicity, Lady Canforth, has had eight long years to regret that she sent her husband from a cold marriage bed to face brutal combat, danger and hardship. The only child of elderly parents, Felicity came to marriage innocent and ignorant, and unable to conceal her shock at the sensual power of the earl's caresses. Before she found the nerve to offer Canforth a more generous welcome, he was called away to war. The Major left behind a countess who was a bride, not a wife; a woman unsure of her husband's feelings, and too timid to confess how fervently she desires the man she wed.

Fate has granted an older, wiser Felicity a second chance to win her husband's heart. Now nothing will stop her from claiming victory over the famous war hero. This Christmas, she'll deploy every ounce of courage, purpose and passion to seize the life and love she's longed for, ever since Canforth left to serve his country. Whatever it costs, whatever it takes, she'll lure the dashing Major back into her bed, where she means to show him he's the only man she wants as her lover —and her love.

After years of yearning and separation, will a Christmas miracle heal the wounds of the past and offer the earl and his bride a future bright with love?

A Match Made in Mistletoe

A mistletoe wish...

All her life, Serena Talbot has been in love with the handsome boy next door, Sir Paul Garside. She always eagerly looks forward to Paul's visit to her family over the Festive Season, even if he usually brings along his dark, sardonic friend Lord Hallam. This year, Serena is determined that Paul's kiss under the mistletoe will lead to a proposal. Even if she has to enlist every ounce of Christmas magic she can get her hands on to make that happen.

But the mistletoe gets it wrong!

When Serena slips a sprig of mistletoe from the village kissing bough under her pillow, it's not Paul who turns up in her dreams as the man she's going to marry, but brooding, intense, annoying Giles Farraday, Marquess of Hallam. Still more annoying, once everyone arrives for the annual Christmas house party, she can't stop watching Giles, and thinking about Giles. And kissing Giles, whether there's mistletoe about or not. Now Paul wants to marry her, and Giles wants to seduce her–and Serena has a bone to pick with the old wives who came up with all this superstitious nonsense in the first place.

9 781925 980912